To Sue,

THE CUS
OF STORIES

AND OTHER TALES FROM
The Book of Reasons

BY
BOB STONE

Be careful what you
wish for.

Beaten Track
www.beatentrackpublishing.com

CONTENTS

THE CUSTODIAN
OF STORIES

1.

YOU MAY HAVE dreamed about the Town. On those nights when you go to bed tired and anxious, you may have visited a town you have never seen before. In your dream, you know the place, though. You are familiar with its granite-cobbled Square, with its hotels on two sides and its Town Hall, built out of the same granite that is under your feet. You have walked its streets and visited its shops. You know that the Town is on the coast because you have strolled along the bush-lined cliff paths. There must be a beach or a bay below, but you may never have seen it. It doesn't matter what other dreams you have, what horrors or dramas await you on other nights; nothing ever happens when you visit the Town. It is a safe place, a quiet place, and you are content and happy there.

When you wake, you will probably wonder where the Town is. You will search your memory, trying to identify when it was that you visited this place and why it made such a lasting impression on you. You will think back to the holidays your parents took you on when you were a child, to the towns and villages you stopped at along the way. You will almost certainly draw a blank. You can recall the dreams in which you drove to the Town. You know where you take a right turn off the main road, and you know where the main road will lead if you don't. You know what the roads look like as they lead into the Town and where the car park is. You are able to visualise clearly the car park itself, with its rows of parking spaces separated by neat lines of small shrubs.

But there is something that you can't picture, and that is what is on the green road signs that direct you to the Town. You can see the signs themselves, and once you have started your waking quest to determine where the Town is, you will concentrate and attempt to see what is written on those signs, so that you can locate this Town on a map and visit it while you are awake, not just while you are asleep. You will concentrate hard, but you will fail. There are words there, but a strange kind of mental illiteracy means that you are unable to read the signs. It is as if your mind doesn't want you to find out where the Town is.

Unable to locate the Town, you will content yourself that at least you will still visit it in your dreams, and who knows? One day, you might be driving to somewhere you have never been before, and you will realise that you are on a familiar road, that there will be a right-hand turn soon. You will drive down roads you recognise and end up in a town you have not previously been to but know very well.

You hope that one day you will come home.

2.

THERE WAS A very good reason why nobody who dreamed about the Town could ever see its name, and that was because it didn't actually have one. The Custodian, who was the Town's sole human occupant, had tried on many occasions to think of a name for the place, but all the names he could think of were either already taken by real places he had been to or heard of, or just sounded silly. Eventually, he had given up, and now he thought of it as The Town, or simply 'here', which suited it quite well considering that for the foreseeable future, he wasn't likely to be living anywhere else.

Although the Custodian was the only human resident of the Town, he was never entirely on his own. There was the man in the newsagent's, which was downstairs in one of the shops, who provided the Custodian with the magazines and comics he liked to read. There was presumably a ground floor to this shop, but the Custodian never needed it, so he had no idea what was there. He obtained his food supplies from the lady in the grocer's, which was often a few doors down from the newsagent but was sometimes in a different street entirely. It didn't matter really; the Custodian always knew where it was when he needed it. These shops, along with the bookshop and the café, supplied the Custodian with all he needed most of the time, and the staff provided him with temporary company if ever he was looking for it. They were there when he needed them to be, but he had no knowledge of where they were when he didn't, if they were anywhere at all.

There were things that you needed to know and there were things that you didn't need to know. It had taken the Custodian a while, but he was beginning to understand the difference between the two.

One thing he had puzzled about for some considerable time was how the Town worked, the physics of it and the logic of it. He had tried to make sense of it over and over again in the early days but had come to the conclusion that there was no sense to be made; things just were the way they were. Once he had decided that this was all he needed to know, he stopped bothering and got on with what he had to do. The Town didn't work using any kind of science or rationale he had ever come across, but he had encountered some pretty weird things before, and the place he now called home was another one of those. Call it magic, call it whatever you want, the Town provided him with everything he could possibly wish for except one thing. He had no company. The people who appeared in the shops and the strange little things he called the elves, although that wasn't what they were, were not human so didn't count. He had no *human* company.

The Custodian had decided to make his home in one of the hotels that bordered the Town Square. When he had first arrived in the Town and understood that he was the only living being there, the plan had been to stay temporarily in the Hotel, to make it a base while he explored. The Town had houses, of course, in the streets that ran off the town centre, and he had initially thought that he might find one of those to live in, but when he had gone to look around, all the houses seemed to be occupied. He saw lights on in windows, and occasionally shadows shifted behind lit curtains, as if people were moving around inside. They never came out, and he came to realise that the houses might not be occupied in this aspect of the Town, but there were probably other versions of the Town, maybe many, and he was seeing echoes of them.

It didn't seem right to move into a house that was somebody's home in any version of the Town, so he stayed in the Hotel. He had a large suite that took up one side of the second floor and was easily big enough for his purposes. The windows gave him a very good view of the Town and meant that if any threat ever approached, as he had been told it might, there was a better chance of seeing it coming.

Once he realised that Pretend People, as he liked to call them, could be brought into being to attend to his needs, he had decided that a receptionist on the Hotel desk during the day and a night porter might be appropriate, even though there was nothing for them to do, as he was the Hotel's only resident. But they were there to chat to from time to time; they were company of a sort. He wondered if he could have given them the faces and personalities of some of the people he missed and had been tempted to try but decided against it. They would not be those people, and he couldn't cope with spending his time with fake versions of the people who had been important to him before he took on this role, especially one. He definitely couldn't cope with a fake version of *that* one. So he made a receptionist he called Harold and a night porter called Joanne because he didn't know anybody with those names. They also didn't look like anybody he knew, although there might have been fleeting resemblances to actors he had seen in a film once. It is very hard to create a human face from scratch, especially when you aren't used to it, so the inspiration had to come from somewhere. They existed purely so that he would have someone to talk to when he needed it. The elves, who weren't elves, had no conversation; they appeared around corners or sometimes out of the drains and spoke in cryptic warnings. The Custodian had not yet learned what these meant.

Although the Custodian was alone and yearned at times for real human company, he wasn't bored. He had his job to do, and that often kept him very busy indeed.

The Custodian had not had a job before this, but he imagined that many people who did have jobs would have been in a similar situation to the one in which he was now. You are given a job to do, and you think the job description tells you all it will entail, but once you start doing it, you discover there is a great deal more to it than you had been told. That was certainly the case here, and if he had known what he would be expected to do, he might have thought twice about accepting the job, but then he had been given no choice in the matter. He had been instructed to look after the thing that he had hidden in the cellar of the Hotel and thought that his responsibility would end there. He had not been told that he would be responsible for the stories of so many people.

That was not the job Joey Cale thought he was accepting when he agreed to be the Custodian of *The Book of Reasons*.

3.

J OEY CALE HAD not been presented with any alternative to living out the rest of his days as Custodian to *The Book of Reasons*. From the moment he was born with a hole in his tiny heart, his destiny had been determined. The hole had been repaired in part by skilled surgeons, but also with a small degree of intervention by a being Joey would later come to know as Remick. A seed of power had been sown in his chest, and when that power had enabled Joey to defeat Saunders, the previous Custodian, who had been corrupted by the very book he was protecting, he was supposed to destroy *The Book* too. He hadn't and now had the permanent job of guarding *The Book* from the world, and in doing so, guarding the world from *The Book*. He had been brought to the Town and left here without an instruction manual. He had to make it up as he went along.

Joey had learned very early on that one of the rules of this place was that he only had to wish for something and he would find it. Sometimes he had to look a bit harder, but it would be there somewhere. He had discovered this particular facility when he had only been in the Town a matter of hours. He had already established that the Town was not populated. He had been left in the middle of the Square, clutching *The Book*, and was immediately aware of the silence. According to the sky, it was probably somewhere around the middle of the day and the Town Square, even of a small place like this, should have been full of people going about their business, but there was nobody.

It was not the first time Joey had been on his own in a world devoid of people; he hadn't liked it much last time and liked it even less now, because last time he had discovered that he was not totally alone. He had met other people, and the lack of one of them in particular was almost too much to think about because it had left a void in his heart that made it hard to breathe. *This* Town was deserted. There was nobody in the Square, nobody on the streets surrounding the Square, nobody in the shops or the hotels. No birds sang; no cats crept around street corners and ambled across the road; no dogs barked. The Town was empty and silent.

It was while he was checking the second of the hotels that it occurred to him that he was hungry. He couldn't remember the last time he had eaten anything, and with no expectations at all, he picked up a bar-food menu from one of the tables. Wistfully, he read the constituent parts of the all-day breakfast the menu advertised and realised that he would never have such a meal unless he cooked it for himself, and that thought led him to wonder where exactly he would buy the ingredients and where he might cook them. There was no one to ask.

This all made a cooked breakfast the most desirable meal he could possibly imagine, and it was this yearning which he initially thought explained the unmistakable aroma of fried bacon which seemed to be emanating from somewhere behind him. He dismissed it at first as a cruel trick of his imagination, but the smell was so strong that it made him turn. One of the tables had been laid with a tray of condiments, cutlery and a large plate on which was the biggest cooked breakfast Joey had ever seen. He didn't question it straight away; he simply sat down at the table and began to devour the food. It was only when he pushed away the plate that he had nearly but not quite managed to clear, that it even occurred to him to wonder where it had come from. He had not seen or heard anybody. There was no kitchen noise coming from anywhere. He had wanted the meal and it had appeared.

Joey didn't really want to use the phrase 'as if by magic', but for want of a better explanation, it would have to do. He had seen plenty of bizarre things recently, so the idea that the best breakfast you'd ever had could appear just by wanting it was surprisingly easy to believe. While he sat and digested his meal, he wondered what else he could do. He had not got any further than deciding whether to try and conjure up a cup of tea or a cup of coffee to follow, however, when *The Book*, which he had tossed a little too carelessly onto the seat next to him, suddenly made its presence felt.

4.

A T FIRST, IT felt like some peculiar kind of itch at the back of his brain, a phantom feeling that made him jerk his head as if a fly had landed on his ear. There was a noise, too, a scratching, rustling noise, soft and just on the edge of his hearing. Years earlier, his parents had rented a cottage for a week in Anglesey. It was a converted farm building and had probably inherited some of the building's former inhabitants because sometimes, in the peace of the evenings, they could hear a slight scuffling sound behind the skirting boards. It was so quiet and brief that you were never sure if you had heard it or not, but it left Joey's mum in fear of waking up one morning to find the cottage overrun with mice, or worse. It was one tiny sound that ruined a holiday.

The sound Joey heard now reminded him of that; it was there and then it was gone, and he wasn't quite sure he had heard it at all. He tried to ignore it and concentrate on the cup of coffee he had decided was the thing he desired most. It should, perhaps, have taken him longer to adjust, but he wasn't at all surprised when a steaming mug of freshly ground coffee was right there on the table in front of him. That it was in the TARDIS-shaped mug he always used at home was a nice touch. He *was* surprised, however, when, just as he was lifting the mug to his lips to have a drink, *The Book* slid off the seat next to him and landed on the carpet with a soft thud. The rational part of Joey's brain suggested that he and *The Book* were on a padded banquette, and maybe he had moved and made *The Book* fall, but the more emotional part of his brain said *I didn't move, it's alive*. He shut out the fear that was making his stomach churn and leaned over to pick *The Book* up.

As he lifted *The Book* off the carpet, he noticed that the catch on the leather strap which kept the covers from opening, and which had been firmly fastened as long as it had been in his possession, was half open. Joey was filled with a sudden, burning desire to open *The Book*, to read it. There were stories in there, tales to get lost in, and he wanted nothing more than to read them all and be consumed by them. With a supreme effort of will, he fought down this desire and pushed the catch firmly back into place. He had experienced reading just a small part of *The Book* before and nearly lost his mind.

"No you don't," he said out loud. "You don't get me like that," and that was when he knew he had to find a safe place to put *The Book*, somewhere out of harm's way, where it could not get into his head.

The solution presented itself as soon as Joey walked out of the bar, holding *The Book* gingerly at arm's length. He was rapidly beginning to understand that in this town, you didn't have to go far to find what you were looking for. Just outside the glass-panelled double doors of the bar, there was another door in the wall, which he was sure he hadn't noticed before. The red warning sign on it read CELLAR – NO ACCESS TO THE PUBLIC, and that looked just about perfect. He had expected that the door would be locked because if you don't want people to get curious about somewhere they shouldn't go, that is generally what you do, but when he tried it, it opened easily. On the other side was a staircase leading down into the darkness, but there was a light switch on the wall at the top of the stairs, which worked, of course, and a bulb somewhere below provided just enough illumination to make the rickety wooden staircase slightly less hazardous. Holding *The Book* in one hand and the stair rail in the other, Joey descended.

The stairs seemed to go on forever. Joey reached at least twenty before he lost count and gave up. Eventually, his foot jarred as it hit solid ground, and he could see the source of the light: a single, dim bulb hanging from a fitting which looked like it should have been condemned decades ago. The cellar itself was quite a large space, its walls lined with empty crates and boxes, which, judging by the dust on them, had not contained the crisps they advertised since long before Joey was born. There was another source of light, too, coming from one corner, the flickering orange glow of flames from a glass panel in the front of an ancient boiler. Joey's first instinct was to see if he could open the panel and throw *The Book* into the flames, but he had been told to guard it, not incinerate it, so instead, he placed it on the floor at the base of the boiler, as if he were warning it *any more trouble and in you go.* Then he hurried back up the stairs and turned off the light. As he shut the door behind him, he thought, *I could really do with finding the key and locking that.* It was not completely unexpected that he heard a click from the door, and when he tried the handle, he found the door had locked itself. He gave the handle one more tug for good measure and, satisfied, left the bar.

5.

Wᴵᴛʜ *Tʜᴇ Bᴏᴏᴋ* safely shut away in the cellar, Joey knew that the Hotel would have to be his residence, at least for now. He roamed the corridors on the various floors until he found a door that felt right and tried the handle. Apparently, he did not need a key-card in this hotel; the door opened with the slightest push, and when he walked into the suite, he knew why it had felt right. It consisted of a large living area with more settees than Joey could ever possibly need and a bedroom with a bed so big that his own bed at home would have fitted into it three times. A door from the bedroom led into a huge bathroom.

He spent a quarter of an hour wandering around the suite looking at things. He tried each of the settees in turn, lay on the bed, washed his face in the bathroom and even boiled the kettle for a cup of coffee. He didn't really want coffee but had decided he was going to have one just because he could. Now he had made the decision as to where he was going to live, he went to explore the Town, but not before he had sent a thought to the room that it would be quite handy if there was a change of clothes or two in the wardrobe when he got back. He knew without question that nobody would need to check his size.

It was as he left the Hotel that he saw for the first time one of the creatures he would come to think of as elves. It appeared out of a vent at the bottom of the wall and seemed so out of place that Joey wasn't sure he was really seeing it at all. It was no more

17

than a foot tall, humanoid in shape but appeared to be carved out of stone or possibly shell and climbed out of the vent with jerky movements that reminded Joey of some of the old films his dad had made him watch in which creatures were brought to life with what his dad had called 'stop-frame animation' or something. They were nothing like the special effects Joey was used to, but he liked them, especially the skeletons in *Jason and the Argonauts*.

The creature he was looking at now landed on the pavement in front of him and stepped back in an almost comic gesture of surprise. It regarded Joey briefly and then, in a quiet, tinny voice, said something which might have been "Don't take it in," or maybe even "Don't take its skin," and then scampered off up the street, leaving Joey unsure exactly what part of his imagination he had conjured *that* from. He shook his head, wondering what other surprises the Town had to offer.

Even this fleeting glimpse of life made Joey feel very much alone. Back in his own world, he had, ironically, apart from one good friend, been something of a loner. He didn't mind his own company then, preferring it to the company of most people he knew. Since then, he had made some good friends and grown especially close to one person in particular, and stranded in the peculiar town, he felt lonelier than he had at any other time in his life. He really should have been prepared for the wish-fulfilment powers of the Town to pick up on this and do something about it, but he was still surprised when he passed a café on one of the roads that led off the Square and saw that the lights were on. He could have sworn the café had been in darkness only seconds earlier, almost as if it was one of those places where the lights are operated by a movement sensor.

Joey peered through the window and was immediately tempted to go in, but there didn't seem much point. The café was deserted, no customers, no staff. If there was someone serving in there, he might have called in for a cup of coffee, but he didn't really fancy it himself. Before he could complete the thought that started *I wonder…* there was suddenly someone standing behind the counter, a young man, maybe his twenties, with a beard which looked like the first he had ever tried to grow, and the shadow of tattoos up his right arm. He looked vaguely familiar, but at the same time, Joey knew it wasn't anyone he had ever met before. Perhaps he had been reminded of someone he had seen in another café at some point. Whoever he was, Joey decided that some company was better than no company at all.

The young man behind the counter looked up and smiled as Joey came in.

"Good afternoon," he said pleasantly, and before Joey could even reply, he had placed a cup of coffee on the counter, strong with a touch of milk in it, just the way Joey liked it.

"Hi," Joey replied. "Thank you."

"No problem."

"Not a bad afternoon," Joey remarked, for want of anything better to say, seeing as the man obviously had no intention of asking for any money.

"Not bad at all."

Joey waited to see if any more conversation was forthcoming. When it wasn't, he took his coffee and went to sit at one of the spotlessly clean tables and drank as quickly as he could. He said goodbye to the café guy as he left and received a vague wave in return. Next time he produced someone out of thin air, he thought, as the café lights went off, he would try and give them a bit more personality.

He failed on his next two attempts, too. The man in the newsagent's was altogether too sarcastic, and the woman in the grocer's was at times painfully jolly, but at least they provided him with some sort of human contact. By the time he had brought Harold and Jo in the Hotel to life, he was getting rather better at it. They both had pleasant, friendly personalities and were happy to chat to Joey for ages about things that interested him. But apart from them and the elves with their dark, obscure threats, Joey saw nobody else for weeks, not until he learned that guarding *The Book* wasn't his only task. The other *would* involve human contact, but of a much more delicate and difficult kind.

6.

THE DAY JOEY learned about his other role began much like any other. He had breakfast in the Hotel bar (just cereal and toast—after a few days of cooked breakfasts, he'd decided that even though this world didn't work like any other, his body still did, and a cooked breakfast every day would be no good at all for his waistline) and had called in to the newsagent to pick up a Doctor Who magazine and some uncalled-for snide remarks about his trousers. Returning to his room, he settled in for a read.

These were his days now, some reading, some wandering around (he had been trying for days to find the road which led out of the Town, just out of interest, but every road he took seemed to lead back to the Square) and the occasional visit to the cellar to make sure *The Book* was behaving itself. He foresaw a time very soon when he would be bored out of his mind and try to come up with new things to do to entertain himself. All the same, he had woken up that morning with a strange feeling that there was something different about the day. It wasn't anything to be apprehensive about, nor was it anything particularly momentous. It was just *something*, and he couldn't put his finger on it.

He found out what it was when a sudden pain ripped into his forehead and the widescreen television flickered on without him touching the remote. That was nothing unusual in itself. The TV had an uncanny knack of knowing which sci-fi show, and indeed which episode, he fancied watching, often before he knew it himself, although he had not yet discovered whether it was capable of showing anything else. He had wondered briefly whether he could find the news or something that would tell him if he was anywhere in the world he had left, but he knew deep down he wasn't. Any time he tried to think the television into showing him something of that kind, the picture dissolved into an angry burst of static that resolved into one of the cartoons he used to watch avidly when he was a child. It was trying to tell him something, but he wasn't sure what.

This time, though, the picture on the screen wasn't static or any show he had ever seen before. It had the feel of one of the shows he hated but his mum loved—so-called 'reality' shows that were not about any kind of reality Joey wanted to be part of, or the shows where fame-hungry idiots were followed around by cameras operated by people who didn't have a very steady hand. The way they were filmed made Joey feel seasick, and the people on the shows just made him sick.

The view on the screen was shot from above and looked down onto a young woman sitting on the edge of a bed in what looked like a small flat, and Joey somehow knew her name was Hannah and that she was staring at a message on her phone. For a moment, that was all he knew. Then, without warning, Joey's head filled with Hannah's story.

7.

HANNAH REGAN HAD fallen for Johnny Haig the moment she saw him. She was having drinks in the pub after work with Jane, Lynn and Mel because it was Friday and it had been a long week. It was Mel's birthday next week, but she was going on holiday with her husband and kids on Sunday and wouldn't be here, so this was the only chance they had to celebrate. Mel didn't want to be out late, though, as she had to take the kids to swimming quite early on Saturday morning.

Hannah was glad she didn't have kids, or indeed anyone to have kids with. They had said it would only be a couple of drinks, but after Mel had gone, Hannah and Lynn, probably Jane, too, would end up making a night of it, and Hannah would end up sending Dom a few drunken texts. Dom was used to it and had said once that he quite looked forward to his Friday 'pissed texts'. He was the sort of friend you didn't find every day.

The girls were on their second round of drinks when Hannah spotted a group of men who had just come into the bar. There were three of them, all wearing suits and obviously straight out of the office. Two were slightly older, but the one Hannah really noticed was around her own age and somehow didn't fit with the other two, who carried too much weight for their suits. One was bald in the way men of a certain age sometimes are when they don't want anyone to know they're losing their hair, and it might have been the lights in the bar, but Hannah was convinced the other one's hair was dyed. There was definitely something not quite natural about it. But the younger man was different. His suit fitted him perfectly, and his dark hair was just the right side of long. Hannah thought he was gorgeous.

Lynn had noticed him too and nudged her. "He's new. I think we'd have noticed him before."

"I've not seen him," Hannah said, trying to sound like she wasn't bothered.

"Pity his mates are knobheads. You'll have to find someone else."

"He's not my type."

"Oh, get lost, Han. He's *exactly* your type. He's definitely mine, anyway."

"Everyone's your type, Lynn." Hannah laughed. "They just need a pulse."

Lynn launched into a story about the new lad in accounts who'd ended up locking himself in the toilets for half an hour, but Hannah had heard it before and wasn't paying attention. She kept stealing glances at the man at the bar. His two friends were roaring with laughter at something, and he was smiling politely but looked bored and possibly even a little embarrassed by them. She picked up her phone and took a selfie but aimed it so she included a view of the dark-haired man over her shoulder. She sent it to Dom with a message.

```
The guy at the bar.
What do you think? x
```

She knew she wouldn't have long to wait for a reply. Dom didn't often go out on Friday nights. Sure enough, a message came straight back.

```
He's okay if you like that sort of
thing. Go for it. The way you look,
he won't stand a chance x
```

Hannah sent back a laughing emoji and a heart. Dom could always make her smile. She looked at the picture she'd sent and wondered what Dom had seen in it. She looked the way she always looked when she went out for Friday drinks. Nothing special. She was wearing a new top, but it was a work top—admittedly a Friday work top with going out at the end of the day in mind—and she had a little more make-up on than she wore for work, but otherwise, she was just Hannah. She glanced at the man at the bar again but had to look away quickly because he was staring in her direction. *Probably looking at Lynn*, she thought, and then realised Mel was talking to her.

"Come on, Han," she said. "It's your round. I'll just have this one and then I'll have to get off."

Hannah looked at the bar, which was starting to get busy. There was a space, but it was right next to the dark-haired man. With no choice, Hannah ran a hand through her hair, picked up her bag and went to the bar, her eyes fixed straight ahead, willing herself not to look at the dark-haired man. It was just her luck that the staff were busy at the other end of the bar. It looked like she was going to have to wait. She stood at the bar and kept her gaze on the bottles behind it, as if she was fascinated by the astonishing range of craft gins the place had to offer, but it didn't work. He spoke to her anyway.

"It's funny how you go invisible, isn't it?"

Turning her head, she discovered the dark-haired man was smiling at her. Up close, he was even better-looking. His face had a light stubble and a fading summer tan, and his eyes were a deep brown. His smile showed teeth that could have been used as an advert for his dental hygienist.

"Sorry?" was the most dazzling, witty response Hannah could come up with.

"At the bar. You go through work all day not getting a moment's peace, but as soon as you stand at the bar, you go invisible."

"Oh! Yes. I do anyway."

"I don't know why they wouldn't notice you," he said. "I did."

Hannah, who had fair skin and blushed easily, hoped to God that the lights were dim enough for him not to see that she was doing it now. They were interrupted by one of the man's colleagues slapping a hand on his shoulder.

"We're off to The Mound, Johnny. You coming?"

"I'm going to have another one here. I'll catch you up."

"I can see why." The other man laughed, clapping Johnny on the shoulder again.

"Fuck off, Gaz," Johnny said, though not unpleasantly, shrugging him off.

Johnny didn't catch up with his colleagues, and Hannah didn't go back to her friends, apart from taking the drinks over. They spent the rest of the night talking and laughing together. Johnny, whom Hannah now knew was Johnny Haig, had recently started working at an office several buildings away from her own and hated his colleagues and the way they pretended to be younger than they were. He had only come out to be sociable, he said, and had really wished he hadn't until he saw Hannah. Hannah was flattered but pleased because Johnny looked so sincere when he said it.

They chatted about their interests and found they had plenty in common. It became a running joke that every time Hannah mentioned a film or a band she liked, Johnny would laugh and say, "This is mad! That's one of my favourites, too!"

When the time came to leave, Hannah was aware that the evening had flown by and she had drunk far less than she would have done if she'd stayed with the girls. Johnny saw her to a taxi and, just before she got into it, handed her a business card.

"My number," he said. "See you around, Hannah Regan."

From the taxi, Hannah sent Dom a message.

`He's lovely. He gave me his number x`

Hannah was almost back at her flat before Dom's reply dropped in.

`Happy for you. Night, hun`

It took Hannah a week to decide whether to contact Johnny. She would have asked Dom's advice, but he must've been busy at work, as he wasn't texting as often as usual. Instead, she did as she often did and concluded that fate would decide for her. It did, the following Friday, when she went out to grab a sandwich for her lunch and found that the usual sandwich shop was unusually busy. Pressed for time, she went to a different shop over the road, and her heart nearly stopped when she saw Johnny standing in front of her in the queue. By the time she left the shop with her smoked salmon bagel, they'd arranged that she would be giving Friday night drinks with the girls a miss and going out with Johnny instead.

That night, he kissed her before she got into her taxi and Hannah's life changed immediately. Friday nights—and several others during the week—now became nights with Johnny instead of the girls, and she spent a lot more of her time texting Johnny rather than Dom. Dom, bless him, was always there for her and seemed pleased she was so happy.

***

It was four months before things began to go wrong.

Hannah was in love with Johnny, and he said he loved her, too. They usually spent one or two nights a week together in her flat, as Johnny had a flatmate he didn't like and didn't want to take Hannah back there. In bed, Johnny was all Hannah had hoped he would be, gentle and considerate, and she wanted him to move out of his flat and in with her, but he was on a lease he couldn't break just yet. He was great company when they were out, funny and attentive, and Hannah found it easy to envisage a future with him. Then came the man in the leather jacket and everything changed.

Hannah hadn't noticed the scruffy-looking man in the corner of the bar until Johnny excused himself to go to the toilet but stopped to talk to him on his way past. They had a brief exchange, and the man followed Johnny through the door to the toilets. He came back out again quickly, and Hannah watched with relief as he left the bar. There was something about him that she didn't like, but Johnny was on such great form when he came back, she forgot all about it.

Two weeks later, the same thing happened again. This time, Hannah couldn't help herself.

"Who was that?" she asked.

"Who was what?"

"That lad you were talking to."

"Just a mate," Johnny said and changed the subject, but there was something about the way he said it that made Hannah uneasy. As he talked, she studied the face she loved for a sign that he was lying, and as she did so, she noticed, with a queasy feeling in her stomach, that there was a fine dusting of white powder under Johnny's nose. It would not have been noticeable to anyone else, but Hannah knew that face so well. Then Johnny blew his nose on a handkerchief, said something about hay fever, and the white was gone.

Later that night, while Johnny slept beside her, she got up, sat on the edge of the bed and sent a message to Dom.

```
I think he's using coke.
I don't know what to do x
```

She was glad Dom wasn't asleep and messaged her back straight away.

```
A  lot  of  people  do,  hun.  It's
everywhere.  As  long  as  he  treats
you  right,  I'd  try  and  ignore  it
for  now.  Here  if  you  need  me  x
```

It was reassuring to know that Dom was there for her. She loved that he was always so calm, but he hadn't really said anything to help. She just wished she knew what to do.

8.

JOEY CALE'S HEAD was filled with Hannah's story. He felt like he had been watching the whole thing through her eyes for hours, but his watch, which was not always completely reliable since he had come to the Town and sometimes seemed to have a mind of its own, told him it had only been minutes. He knew what perfume Hannah's friend Lynn wore, what Dom looked like—even though in the part of Hannah's story he had seen Dom only existed as texts on a screen—and felt the turmoil in Hannah's stomach as she sat on the bed uncertain as to what she should do next. Joey was left feeling incomplete, as if he had been disturbed while reading a good book and would never find out how it ended. He had become so involved in Hannah's life, he needed to find out what happened next.

The television read his mind and sprang back into life. This time, however, what Joey saw was different. It looked for all the world as if someone had pressed a fast-forward button and he was watching a speeded-up silent depiction. He saw Hannah get up, presumably the next morning, and get ready for work. She kissed Johnny goodbye, though it was barely a peck. Joey followed her as she caught the train for a couple of stops and then walked the rest of the way to work. The day at work passed by in seconds, and then she was home again, getting ready to go out.

When Joey caught her face in the bathroom mirror, she looked pale and worried, and then she was in a bar with Johnny, and Joey could only watch in dismay as the lad in the leather jacket made a reappearance. Next, Hannah and Johnny were back at the flat and arguing. Joey could see the hurt in Hannah's face and the fury in Johnny's and watched in mute horror as Johnny's hand drew back and then connected with Hannah's cheek and sent her sprawling backwards onto the bed.

Johnny left, the room darkened to night, and Hannah stayed where she was until the morning. She got up, got changed (Joey averted his eyes) and applied make-up to the mark on her face and left for work, her gaze straight ahead, no life in her eyes. Again, she caught the train again, then started her short walk to the office. Joey could only watch as she stepped into the road and the black Mercedes hit her full on and threw her into the air like a discarded paper bag.

Then the television went black.

Joey sat there staring at the blank screen for a very long time, with a barrage of questions occupying his mind. Why this story? Of all the stories, why had he been made to experience this one? Was it supposed to teach him something? Was there something he was meant to have done? He tried to send out a mental message to whatever forces were controlling his life, asking what his role was in all this. Then the television switched itself back on and gave him the answer.

It showed him Dom's story.

9.

DOMINIC BOOTH HAD loved Hannah Regan for as long as he could remember, or so it felt. He had only known her for four years, yet it seemed as if she had been in his life forever. For at least two of those years, he had loved her but had never told her. Now she had met someone and seemed happy, and he had left it too late.

He had met her when he took a post at the office where she worked through an employment agency. The post was only a temporary contract for a year, but the money was good and it was something to do while he made up his mind about what he actually wanted to do with his life. On his first day, he was assigned a trainer, a gorgeous redhead named Hannah, and he got on with her straight away. Within a very short space of time, he discovered that she had a wicked sense of humour and a sharp intelligence, but she had no real idea how smart or how attractive she was. He also discovered that he had made a friend for life. They chatted easily at work and texted often when they were not in work. They supported each other through bad times and made each other laugh helplessly at other times. When the contract ended and Dom had to move on, they stayed in touch, often having text conversations that went on for hours. Dom sometimes wondered if it wouldn't be easier just to pick up the phone and talk to each other, but at least this way he could pick his words before he sent them and not make a fool of himself by blurting out something unwise.

He knew Hannah cared a great deal about him. She told him so, told him he was her best friend and that she didn't know where she'd be without him. He said the same but never used the word 'love' in case it made everything change and he lost her completely.

Dom had thought a lot about how he would feel if Hannah ever met anyone. To him, it seemed like it would only be a matter of time; after all, if he thought Hannah was beautiful, inevitably other men would. He sat at home on the nights she went out with her friends from work, waiting for her to text him, which she invariably did. She told him about what antics Lynn and the others were getting up to; sometimes she told him about men she had spotted but hadn't talked to and who had shown no interest in her. He always tried to sound sympathetic and not too relieved. Then she met Johnny Haig.

He lived through the first meeting, encouraging her to go for it when she sent him a blurry picture of some long-haired tosser standing at the bar. He supported her through waiting for him to call and her nerves before the first date. In the early stages of the relationship, she had still texted Dom as often as ever, but as she and Johnny began to spend more time together, she sometimes went days without texting at all. When she did text him, always on a night when she wasn't seeing Johnny, he did his best to be pleased to hear from her and to act like nothing had changed between them while still feeling like some kind of consolation prize. On those nights, he chose his words more carefully than ever. He tried hard not to let her know how conflicted he was, torn between jealousy and a genuine desire to be the good friend Hannah deserved and be happy for her.

Now he was sitting in his room at his parents' house, while the TV show carried on without him, staring at his phone and desperately hoping it would buzz with a new message from Hannah but with no clue what he would say if it did. She had just told him Johnny was using cocaine, and, like an idiot, he had encouraged her to ignore it rather than telling her to walk away from the dickhead and do it now. He was, as she had made clear on many occasions, just her friend, and he had no right to tell her what to do. He had sent off his message telling her to turn a blind eye; she'd read it, and now he could only wait to see if she replied. He wished he could help her, but Hannah didn't reply that night.

She didn't reply the next day either. Dom kept checking his phone throughout the morning when work allowed and hoped that maybe she would text during her lunch break. He took his own at 12:30, the time he knew she had hers, and, instead of having a sandwich at his desk, went out of the office in case she needed to speak to him. He didn't feel like eating so went into one of the nearby coffee shops and ordered the strongest black coffee they had. He managed to find a seat in a booth and sipped his drink, his phone on the table in front of him, and waited.

He was still waiting ten minutes later when a voice said, "Is anyone sitting here?" and a young man with untidy brown hair sat down opposite him. Dom didn't reply but waved towards the seat, feeling slightly foolish because the man, who was probably four or five years younger than him, had already sat with a takeaway cup of tea.

"They never call when they say they're going to, do they?" the young man said, pointing towards Dom's phone. "Maybe you should call her."

Dom looked at the young man and was ready to say, "Maybe you should just fuck off and mind your own business," but he caught something in this stranger's expression, a sincerity that, for a second, made him think that whoever this man was, he *knew*.

"Actually," the young man said, "I think I'd better get back. I didn't realise the time. Call her or at least text her, but do it now. Tell her how you feel. Don't leave it too late. Take my

35

word for it—we get little enough time with the ones we love. Don't waste it."

With that, he was gone. Dom picked up his phone and tried to compose the perfect text, the one that would say everything he wanted to say and would leave her in no doubt about how he felt. For once, all his words deserted him, and he knew there was only one thing to do. He typed a few words and pressed send.

```
Hannah, I love you.
Call me xx
```

He had just put his phone down on the table when it rang.

10.

JOEY KNEW THE end of the story. It would be another two weeks before Dom and Hannah went on their first date, but when Hannah got off the phone with Dom, she immediately sent Johnny a text telling him she thought it was best if they didn't see each other anymore. He sent her a very cold reply, just saying 'Fine', which brought tears to her eyes, of sadness at first and then of rage. She deleted his texts and blocked his number and felt nothing but relief. Then she rang Dom, told him she loved him, too, and that it was about time they did something about it, the sooner the better. Joey didn't need to know any more of their story than that. Hannah was going to live and had all she wanted to be happy. What more was there to know?

He sat and stared at the television, which was blank once more, and smiled. If he could use the power he had been given to make a positive difference to people's lives when they needed it, then he was going to enjoy being Custodian. All the same, being able to give Hannah and Dom the chance of a happy ending made him think of what he had given up to do this, and much as he tried to fight it, the thought of Emma forced its way into his mind.

On paper, there was no way anyone could have made a match out of Joey and Emma Winrush. He was the reserved, shy teenager, whose social skills had been hampered by his parents' determination to bubble-wrap his life. She was the rebellious, sarcastic, purple-haired cynic, who did her best with words and deeds to keep everyone at arm's length. Yet when Emma had died at the hands of *The Book*'s previous Custodian, the corrupt bastard called Saunders, Joey's heartbeat had kept her safe and brought her home. Once reunited with her body, Emma had understood the bond between them long before he did. They had admitted their love for each other and shared too few kisses before Joey's destiny as Custodian was revealed and he had left her behind. Now he spent his time trying not to think about her, in case the peculiar properties of this world picked it up as a wish. If he couldn't be with the real thing, he would rather be on his own than be with an Emma made of rememberings and imagination. He hoped she was well and happy, but he also had a job to do.

That night, he had a dream that proved to him that the job was going to be harder than he thought.

11.

J OEY DIDN'T OFTEN dream these days, or at least he didn't recall them if he did. Maybe reality was enough for his brain to cope with without adding any further strangeness. On this night, however, he had one of the most vivid dreams of his life, and it left him sweating and shaken when he woke.

In the dream, he was returning to his suite in the Hotel, and it was nighttime, which was unusual because Joey tended not to go out in the dark if he could help it. The elves seemed to be more prevalent after sundown, and it was disconcerting enough to look at them without having to listen to their obscure mutterings coming out of the darkness. It was definitely dark in his dream because Joey reached out to turn on the lights, but a voice from somewhere in the room stopped him.

"Leave them off." It sounded like someone with the worst sore throat he had ever heard. "My eyes are new and it hurts."

"Who's there?" Joey asked, his hand still on the light switch.

"No one you know. Now leave the lights alone."

Even in a dream state, Joey knew it was a threat and, unable to see whether this stranger was armed, withdrew his hand from the light switch.

"Where are you?" he asked.

"Close enough. Stay there while we talk."

Joey heard a rustling from nearby and could just about make out an indistinct shape in the gloom.

"Talk about what?"

"Stories, Mr. Cale. We need to talk about stories and how you're getting it wrong."

"I don't know what you mean."

"I think you do. You found your way into somebody's life today, into their story, and you changed it. It wasn't your fault, of course. They asked for it, even if they had no idea what they were asking."

"I saved someone's life."

"You saved the life of someone who wasn't supposed to live. That wasn't how the story was supposed to end."

"Who says?"

"Oh, Mr. Cale, you have a great deal to learn. It should have ended with her death because that would make a much better story. That...*mess* you came up with. What was that?" The voice in the darkness snorted. "She lives and goes off with the friend? It was pathetic."

"It was what she wanted," Joey protested. "It made her happy."

"Was it? Was it *really* what she wanted? Why did she go to bars like that? Why was she attracted to that other man? If you're going to do this job, you need to start asking the right questions. You'll learn."

"No. Not if people get hurt."

"You could have stopped her walking in front of the car. It wouldn't have taken much. You could have stopped her and asked her for the time. Her story could have gone a different way. That man would have hurt her over and over again. He would have left her broken and begging for the end, and you could have made it happen."

"Why would I do that?"

"Because it would have hurt her, and that hurt would have fed *me*. You made her story dull, and nobody benefits from that. This power you have? You could have so much more. You could have the power to take anything you want. Feed me and I can make you a god."

"You're *it,* aren't you? You're *The Book.*"

"I am what *The Book* was—and what it could be again if you are prepared to learn."

"No. Never. I will not make people hurt just to feed you. You can stay in the cellar or I'll burn you. The choice is yours. But I will do this job the way I think is right."

Joey felt it then, a touch like old leather on his arm and a puff of stale, dusty breath on his face.

"No. You will do it my way. They always do."

Joey woke up then, his heart beating a syncopated rhythm and his skin clammy with sweat. It was a long time before he could turn the lights on and be sure that he was alone.

12.

T HE NEXT MORNING, as early as he dared, Joey went to the cellar door and wished it to be unlocked. He turned on the light and went down the stairs, half expecting to find that *The Book* had gone or moved or grown legs or something. It hadn't. It was still lying on the cellar floor by the boiler, exactly where he'd left it. He prodded it with the toe of his shoe, and it moved slightly but did nothing else.

"You're just a stupid book," he said and left it where it was. On his way out of the cellar, he nearly stumbled backwards down the stairs when he saw an elf sitting on the edge of one near the top. The creature regarded him with unblinking eyes that almost looked as though they were painted on its head.

"*Flay*," it said.

"Oh, get lost," Joey replied, stepping over it and resisting the urge to kick it down the stairs. He left the cellar and willed the door to lock itself, adding an extra bolt for good measure, and went out into the fresh air. He had a stench of ancient leather in his nostrils and needed to be rid of it.

He didn't return to the Hotel for several hours. He spent the time wandering about, walking down random streets to see if any of them led anywhere other than the Square. When he found once again that none of them did, he went to the grocer's and acquired the makings of a meal—he couldn't say *bought* because even if he had any money, none ever changed hands in the Town. He could have wished his meals into existence but instead had brought the grocer's shop into being, stocked with everything he could want, and cooked his own meals in the Hotel kitchen. It gave him a feeling of normality, routine and, if he was honest, something else to do to fill his time. Until the television had involved him in the stories of Hannah and Dom, he had been bored. There were only so many books you could read or streets you could explore, especially when they all led to the same place. At least cooking different meals gave his days a bit of variety, and the fact that his attempts were not always wholly successful made life a little less predictable than the perfectly cooked and presented meals he had been eating until then.

What had happened with Hannah had changed everything. If he now had the ability to enter other people's lives and change them, in this case for the better, then it gave him a purpose but also a responsibility. The stories Saunders created had populated *The Book of Reasons* and given him unimaginable power, but it had corrupted him and broken his mind. In light of his dream the previous night, it was clear to Joey that *The Book* would try to do the same to him. All he had to do was not let it.

Returning to the Hotel, he dropped off his shopping in the kitchen and then went up to his room, sat in front of the television and waited. He didn't have to wait long.

Over the course of the next few days, he prevented one man's insecurities from ruining the best relationship of his life, helped a small girl reunite with the family cat and persuaded a young woman to destroy the photographs her lecherous boss had sent her and move to another company where a much better manager and rapid promotion awaited her. But for every story he brought to a positive outcome, he had to contend with the shadow figure that embodied *The Book* visiting him in his sleep and ranting or pleading or threatening him, demanding he give the stories different conclusions. The man *should have* carried on being suspicious of his girlfriend until she left him for someone who didn't keep wishing for the end. The little girl *should have* found the mangled corpse of the cat by the side of the road. The harassed young woman should have shown the photographs to her colleagues and the boss's wife, leading to the manager's disgrace, divorce and suicide. Every time *The Book* tried to exert its malign influence on him, Joey stood firm, but every time, he felt a small bit of his resolve eroding.

It was Miles Walker who tested Joey to his limits and nearly forced him into his first mistake. Miles was fifteen years old. He worked hard at school and did his best to make his parents proud. He excelled in many subjects, apart from maths, with which he'd always struggled but still managed to achieve reasonable grades through sheer persistence. In return, he was ignored by many in his class and bullied by others. He had little interest in sports, even though he could outrun most of the school if he wanted. He spent his evenings studying, so could not join in with conversations about the previous night's television. He dressed in the school uniform with no modifications, and his trainers were comfortable and affordable for his parents and of no fixed brand. Miles was bullied for being quiet, for wearing the wrong shoes, for the colour of his skin and for the name his jazz-loving parents had given him. He spent much of his day feeling that no matter what he did or how hard he tried, he could never fit in or do the right thing. He could please his parents or his peers but never both. Knowing that he would not be at the school forever, he elected to please his parents.

The ringleader of the bullying faction was a thick and thickset lad called Kirk McAdam, who was the youngest of three boys. His older brothers, Harrison and Burt (the McAdam parents liked movies as much as the Walkers liked music), had held the title of cock of the school before him, and Kirk was determined to carry on the tradition. He took every opportunity to abuse Miles openly while anyone was listening and in snide, quiet remarks when only

Miles could hear. He carried out his physical assaults in the same way, overt with an audience and sly trips and digs when no one was looking. Miles ignored him as far as he could, always wishing to avoid confrontation, but in enclosed classrooms and corridors, this was not always possible. He tried to get on with his work and keep a low profile while silently wishing that one day Kirk would choke on one of the protein shakes he ostentatiously guzzled despite never actually going to the gym or doing any exercise to back them up.

Miles might have continued to ignore Kirk were it not for Paige. Paige was one of the very few of his classmates who also liked to get on with their work. She kept her head down, but on the rare occasions she raised it, Miles couldn't help but notice how pretty she was. He tried not to let it distract him from his work, but sometimes it just happened. Then the day came when the physics teacher, Mr. Galbraith, paired his students up for a project on lenses, and Miles, inevitably, was paired with Paige. As they worked together, they started to talk to each other, and Miles was delighted to learn that she was just as nice as she looked.

Over the coming weeks, Miles realised that he had found a friend. Unfortunately, this only went to fuel Kirk's bullying, and he began to make loud, suggestive and even overtly sexual remarks. It didn't matter how much Paige advised Miles to ignore him, it became harder and harder to do. The more humiliation Kirk piled on, the more Miles' hatred grew until the day Kirk deliberately barged into Paige in the corridor and knocked her to the floor. That was the day Miles vowed revenge.

The idea of putting weedkiller into Kirk's protein shake came out of nowhere, and once it had entered Miles' head, it wouldn't leave. He began to watch Kirk out of the corner of his eye, trying to determine if there was a pattern to the times the shake was left unattended. Once he established that there was, all he had to do was buy the weedkiller. The following Saturday, when he was out running errands for his mother, he called into the local hardware shop and stood in front of the shelves wondering which one was the best to buy and trying to ignore the boxes of rat poison on the shelf above. As he pondered, he became aware of a young man, perhaps a few years older than he was, standing next to him and also studying the bottles of weedkiller.

"Which one's the best, do you think?" the young man asked.

"I don't know," Miles said. "What's it for?"

"Same as you. Getting rid of an unwanted nuisance. You've got to be so careful with the dose, though. Thing is, Miles, it depends whether you want to make him puke or kill him."

Miles gaped at the young man and then glanced over his shoulder to see where the exit was in case he needed to run.

"I'd use the rat poison, myself," the young man continued. "It's much more effective. He'll never bother you or Paige again. Just make sure you don't get caught."

"Look, I don't know who you are—"

"My name is Mr. Cale. I used to be just like you. I wanted to work and to learn, but it's not easy, is it? You don't need that bastard on your back all the time. Use the rat poison—"

The young man suddenly stopped speaking and winced as if he had the worst ice cream headache ever, then shouted, "No! Miles, get out of here. Don't do this. Just ignore Kirk and learn. Do well. That's the best revenge."

For a moment, Miles froze, watching in confusion as the young man's face contorted with pain, then got out of the shop as quickly as he could. Once he was halfway down the road, he stopped and looked back. No one had seen him. No one had followed. No one would ever know how close he had come to making the biggest mistake of his life.

Miles never carried out his revenge. He took the strange young man's words with him for the rest of his time at the school: *Do well. That's the best revenge.* One of the main factors in him doing well was that two months after Miles failed to buy weedkiller, Kirk used racially aggressive language towards him and was overheard by the headteacher, who was himself of Afro-Caribbean descent and threatened Kirk with a fixed-term exclusion. When he used the same language on the headteacher, the exclusion was made permanent. The other big factor in Miles' success was that Paige stayed by his side, and they supported and encouraged each other. They even tried dating briefly but decided they were better off as friends. On the day he and Paige received their A' Level results, Miles spotted an article in the local paper which told of how one Kirk McAdam had been found dead in the prison cell where he was serving time for drug offences and a racially aggravated assault. *The best revenge,* Miles thought and threw the newspaper in the bin.

13.

JOEY CRASHED BACK into his Hotel suite, skidding across the floor and onto the settee. His brain was on fire and his ears were full of white noise. It felt like insects were crawling in his hair, and he scratched at it frantically, trying to get rid of them. He had come so close. *The Book* had been in his head and he had nearly succumbed to it. He tried to breathe and blot out the noise, and gradually it subsided until all Joey was left with was rage. No more. That was the last time *The Book* would invade his brain. It needed dealing with and right now.

He stormed out of his suite and down the stairs to the cellar door where two elves were lurking. "*Skin*," one said, and the other growled, "*Flay*," and Joey was about to tell the pair of them to fuck off, when he suddenly understood. He had been told by his old friend Remick that *The Book* was bound with the skin of another of his kind who had fallen and been flayed. Joey made a detour to the kitchen, grabbed a set of tongs and one of the sharpest knives he could find and went down the steps to the cellar.

As he approached *The Book*, the white noise started up in his head again. This time, he could hear vague words and curses and threats, but he blocked them out. Snatching *The Book* up off the floor, he inserted the point of the knife into the leather cover.

He had expected something to happen but wasn't ready for the scream that assaulted his mind, and he nearly dropped *The Book*. Forcing himself to ignore the noise, he sliced into the leather, gripped one edge of the slit in each hand and tore the cover from

The Book. It came away in one piece and he hurled it onto the floor. It hissed once, like a furious cat, and then lay there silent.

Clamping the naked book under his arm, Joey used the tongs to pick up the cover, opened the hatch on the front of the boiler and, with barely a hesitation, tossed the ragged leather into the flames. Briefly, the screams tore like fishhooks into his brain, and then were silent. Under his arm, *The Book* vibrated, and a red cloud like thick smoke rushed out from the pages and followed the leather into the fire. The flames flared crimson as Joey slammed the hatch closed.

Tentatively, he opened *The Book* and looked inside: the pages were blank and pristine, waiting for new stories to be written. Satisfied, Joey carried *The Book* out of the cellar and didn't look back.

Safely back in his suite, he sat on the settee, *The Book* on a table next to him. He willed the television to switch on and hoped it would show him the story he wanted to see.

14.

EMMA WINRUSH WAITED with mounting impatience in the queue at the supermarket checkout, wishing she'd used the self-service instead, even though something invariably failed to scan each time she did. She had a remarkable knack for picking the wrong queue, joining what looked like the shortest one but usually turned out to be the slowest.

There were only two people ahead of her, but one was a pensioner who couldn't understand why her expired vouchers couldn't be accepted and then tried to pay using what looked like the contents of several piggy banks. Directly in front of her was a young mother who seemed more concerned about what was on her phone than the fact that the toddler in her trolley was covering its face liberally with chocolate. Emma's tolerance was being tested to its limits. She just wanted to pay for the bread, milk and beans, which were all she could afford until her benefits came on Thursday, and then get the hell out of here, but the fates were conspiring against her. There were days when she hated her life.

She tried so hard not to hate her mother. Some days she could just about manage it, but there were others when she wanted to murder her. Occasionally, she actually thought she would do it, too, but first she'd need to know where the hell her mother was. That was the gratitude Emma received for all the nights she'd spent nursing the woman back to health, all those hours watching her mother pace the house, looking for any bottles Emma might have missed in one of her sweeps, and then pouring out her bile against the daughter who was trying to save her life.

Emma ignored the insults and the curses and held her mother when she needed it. She fed her even when the last thing she wanted was food, sat with her while she slept and waited for the grip of alcohol to loosen. She did all this because she loved her mother and because she carried with her the guilt that, although her mum was dependent on the drink before Emma had disappeared, it had taken over her life since she had been gone.

The guilt was irrational, Emma knew. It wasn't as if she'd left by choice; she'd walked around a familiar street corner and into a nightmarish, deserted world and hadn't been able to find her way back until Joey had abandoned her and sent her home to become an alcoholic's carer, only to be abandoned again when her mother walked out of the house one day, leaving a note full of apologies and no forwarding address. Emma had thought about trying to find her but in the end couldn't be bothered. She was too tired and it was too hard. The only slight ray of sunshine in an otherwise grey sky was that the mortgage was paid, so at least she wasn't homeless. She had no job, no money, no boyfriend and no life, but at least she had a roof over her head. If the worst came to the worst, she could always sell the house.

She walked home from the supermarket and wasn't surprised to find that it was raining; not proper rain, just the sort of drizzle that soaks you. It was that sort of a day.

She unlocked the front door to the house, called out the now habitual, "Hi, Mum! I'm home!" for the benefit of anyone who might be listening and feel inclined to take advantage of a young woman on her own, and went inside.

15.

J OEY STARED AT the television screen, willing it to show him something, anything. Of all the stories he had seen, all the stories he knew he would see, there was only one he wanted right now, but since he had come back to his suite after burning *The Book*'s cover, the television was no longer responding to his will. It would flash on, show him a snippet of someone's life and then return to black. Joey wanted to put his foot through it.

He sat back on the settee and closed his eyes. Maybe he didn't need the television at all. Perhaps that had just been a way of showing him what he could do. He reached out a hand and touched *The Book*.

"Come on," he said. "Let me see her. Just once."

He held that thought in his mind, repeating it over and over and blocking out everything else. He tried to push the thought out of his mind and into reality, and as he did, he felt something give and opened his eyes. There was a blur in the air in front of him.

"Come *on!*" he said, pushing with his mind as hard as he could. And then the blur formed into a picture. She was *there*, letting herself into her house and calling out to her mother.

Joey sagged in relief. She was okay and getting on with her life, and he knew now he could let her go.

16.

THE NOISE IN the cellar started an hour or so later, but by then, Joey had fallen asleep on the settee and heard nothing. It started as a scratching, coming from somewhere inside the boiler, and then the scratching became a knocking, and the sides of the copper tank began to bulge and strain. The welded seam creaked and groaned and then burst. Boiling water poured out of the gash that had opened up in the side of the tank and pooled on the floor. Through the steam, first one, then a second, half- formed hand emerged, gripped the edges of the hole and pulled it wider. Something stepped out of the tank and onto the sodden floor, something which, had he seen it, Joey would have described as a poor attempt to build a large version of one of the elves out of clay. It stretched its misshapen back, and its eyes flashed red with fire.

"You idiot, Cale," it said. "You should have listened. I'll be back for you."

Then, in a flash of scarlet flame, it was gone.

17.

EMMA SET ASIDE the beans on toast that she didn't really want and gazed at the empty room, at her empty life. This was it, now. This was all she had to look forward to.

"Oh, Joey," she said. "I wish you'd come back and take me with you."

18.

J OEY WAS WOKEN by a movement against his palm. At first, he didn't know what it was, but then he realised that he had fallen asleep touching *The Book*, and it was struggling under his hand. He let go, and *The Book* flew open. As he watched, words began to form on the blank page, and he knew with absolute clarity that someone, somewhere, had just called out to him with a wish.

He smiled. There was a new story about to be written.

THE AUTHOR'S TALE

D R. MARKHAM WANTS me to call him Gary, but I can't bring myself to do it. He doesn't look like a Gary. He's got one of those serious, humourless faces, the sort that makes it hard to imagine anyone using a shortened form of his name. He looks, to me at least, more like a James or a Stephen (with a 'ph', definitely not a 'v'). Some people suit their names, and all writers struggle at times to name their characters. You don't want a name you've already used for someone else, and I try to avoid using the names of anyone I know in case they think I'm trying to say something about them. The name Gary has completely different connotations to me and certainly doesn't fit a suited, fussily neat, middle-aged psychotherapist. I don't feel particularly inclined to call him 'Doctor' either, because for all I know, he got his qualification from the internet or somewhere like that. Usually, I try not to call him anything at all.

I sit with my arms folded and my hands hidden in my armpits and do my best to answer his questions. He asks *a lot* of questions, and I'm not convinced he listens to my answers. I try to be as honest as I am able, but he keeps asking the same things, every session. I don't know what he wants from me, what the magic key is that will let me out of here, but I obviously haven't supplied it yet because every week we go through the same routine, then he goes away and I stay here.

"How are you sleeping?" he asks. That is always his first question, and one day I might have a different answer. The truth is, I sleep very little these days. I am woken by ideas laying siege to my mind. Sometimes they are fully formed stories and sometimes they are just fragments, but they all need writing down or they will have eluded me by morning. Writing takes a great deal longer now, because of my hands, so I have to ration myself to three hours' sleep a night, assuming my brain allows me to do so.

"Fine," I tell Markham. "Like a baby." I'm not sure if he realises that I've chosen that expression very carefully. Many new parents will be more than aware of how little sleep their babies allow them to have.

"And you still dream?"

"You go mad if you don't, I believe. We wouldn't want that."

"Do you still feel compelled to write them down?"

"I'm a writer," I reply. "I feel compelled to write *everything* down. That's what I do."

Markham looks at me over his glasses, something nobody else called Gary would do.

"You know what I mean," he says. "I know you've refused before, but I really think it might prove helpful if you let me see some of the things you've written down."

He always tries to catch me out like that, and it never works.

"When they're published," I say, as I do every time, "you can read as many as you like."

He lays the tablet on which he has been pretending to write notes face down on his lap, and I know it is time for The Talk, the one where he pretends that our relationship is friendly rather than professional.

"I'll be honest with you," he says, "I'm not seeing very much progress here. There's nothing I'd like more than to sign your discharge form, but at the moment, I don't see that happening any time soon. I've said this before, but you need to participate fully in your own recovery. There's only a certain amount I can do for you, but I can't if you don't take it seriously."

"I understand," I reply to make him feel better. "But there's only so much I can tell you, and I've already told you most of it."

"Most of it?" I should have known he'd seize on that one word. What kind of a writer is so careless about their choice of words? "Tell me the rest. Tell me about *The Book*. I believe *The Book* started all this, but you still haven't told me much about it. It would be helpful to know where you got it from and what happened to it after you read it."

"I can't tell you that. You know I can't. Surely you understand what *The Book* does. You've seen it. You must see that I cannot risk anyone else finding it. It's far too dangerous."

"So you have said. Often. But you haven't explained how. You won't say what it is, or what it does. It makes me think that this book, if such a thing ever existed, is just that. A book. Everything else comes from your imagination."

"I'm a writer," I say testily. "Everything I write comes from my imagination. But that's how *The Book* works if you really want to know. It puts things in your imagination. It invades your imagination. It makes you imagine things you couldn't conceive of imagining before. Imagine a masquerade ball where none of the guests has a face under their mask, or a dog with sapphire eyes, or a world with no concept of maths."

"I can't," Markham concedes. "I don't understand any of those things."

"Well, I can. I imagine things like that all the time. *All* the time."

For a moment or two, there is silence. Markham still hasn't turned his tablet over. He looks defeated and sad.

"All right," I say. "I'll show you some of what I've been writing. I've been transcribing the stories I read in *The Book*. What I've written is drawn from memory and dreams, so I hope that I've diluted the stories enough for them to be safe. I'll let you read them, but every story has a warning contained within it, and it's always the same. Be careful what you wish for. Your wish

may be granted, but there is always a price that must be paid.
Remember that and remember that you wished to read my
writing. Maybe it will help you understand why I have to write
these things down, why I write and write until my hands are like
this. It is what I wished for."

As I speak, I take my hands out from under my armpits and show
them to him in all their twisted, bruised agony.

"I only hope that whatever your price is, it is not too dear for
you to afford."

PLENTY

B
ILLY KING WAS not an alcoholic. Certainly, he liked a
drink, in much the same way as everyone likes a drink. He
stood at the bar in the King's Head most nights but always
left when he knew he'd had enough. Besides, there wasn't much to
keep him home since Sheila had left and there was never anything
on the television. It was his social life and it did no one any harm.
It wasn't as if he spent every night sitting at home throwing whisky
down his throat. He liked a drink, but nobody could say he had
a problem. He always had Sundays off, too, unlike the other lads,
who spent most of the day there. Billy usually tidied his small
house on a Sunday and did the shopping.

Nobody at the King's Head thought Billy had a drink problem,
mainly because they spent a similar amount of time there.
If Billy had a problem, they all did. There was Harry, and there
was Tommy No-Legs, who was wheeled in by a carer who left
him there and came back later. There was Stavros the Greek
(who wasn't Greek and wasn't called Stavros either) and the man
with the dog, whose name Billy had never caught but who sat
at the same table every night, feeding crisps to his border collie.
Billy had never caught the dog's name either, but it lay under the
table as good as gold while its master and Billy and the others
talked about football and politics and eyed the young talent that
paraded in the bar before going on to nightclubs. They all drank
a few pints each while they talked, sometimes finishing with

a couple of shorts on a Saturday, then went home to their various houses and didn't see each other again until the next night.

Billy very rarely thought about the money he was spending. He worked all day and was entitled to spend his wages any way he wanted. He always had enough to eat and paid his bills more or less on time. He had no one to please but himself, no one to notice or care what time he got home. He had a few drinks and a chat and a laugh and did no harm to anyone.

The King's Head rarely attracted strangers; it just wasn't that kind of pub. It was tucked away down a side street by the canal, and so it was difficult to come upon by chance. Visitors to the town usually went in the Railway or the Albert on the High Street because when you went shopping, you would find it hard to miss them. The King's Head was well hidden, and if you weren't from the area, you would never know it was there. So it came as a surprise to Billy when he met a stranger at the bar one June evening. The stranger was well dressed, youngish, looked like a city type and was completely out of place in the King's Head, but he seemed quite relaxed as he stood at the bar, a pint in his hand. When Billy ordered his pint, the stranger nodded to him.

"Good pint," he said.

"It's not bad," Billy replied.

"No," the stranger went on pleasantly, "I know my beer and this is a good pint. Nice pub, too. Very quiet. I'm new to this area, and I only found it by accident."

"It's my local," Billy told him.

"I thought it might be. I bet you've sunk a fair few pints in here over the years."

"One or two," Billy answered cautiously. He was suddenly not sure if he liked the way the conversation was going.

"Good," the stranger said with a beaming grin. "Any man who likes his beer is fine with me. The thing is, I like my pint, too.

But the doctor's told me I can't have any more. Liver trouble, he said. This is my last one."

With that, he raised his pint to Billy. It was only then that Billy noticed what the stranger was drinking out of. It was a tankard made of pewter or possibly even silver, with an elaborate pattern engraved on the side. The handle was carved out of what looked like bone.

"Be a shame to waste that tankard," Billy said before he could stop himself.

"What, this?" The stranger looked at the tankard in what seemed to be surprise. "I've had it for years." He set it down on the bar so they could both look at it.

"What's the handle?" Billy asked. "Some sort of bone?"

"I don't really know. I'll tell you a funny thing, though. The bloke I bought it off swore it was made out of horn. And not just any horn. He reckoned it was made from the Cornucopia."

"The what?"

"The original Horn of Plenty. It was supposed to never run dry."

Billy looked at the stranger for a moment, trying to figure out whether the other man was making fun of him, but he didn't seem to be.

"That's just a story, though, isn't it?" Billy said.

"Well, of course it is!" The stranger grinned broadly. "The bloke who sold it to me was old, you know? Not the full shilling. He'd have said anything to get a sale. I just bought it because I like it. Although … it's probably just my imagination, but I don't seem to have paid for as many pints since I had this."

The stranger took another sip of his beer.

"I'll tell you what," he said, licking the foam from his lips, "because you like your beer and I can't have it anymore, *you* can have the tankard!"

Billy said nothing for a second or two, wondering what the catch was. In his experience, sudden, unexpected generosity usually had a catch somewhere. As if reading his mind, the stranger said, "Don't look so worried. I'm only trying to give it a good home. And I like you. I can't think of a better home for my old friend. We've been through thick and thin, me and this tankard, and I'd hate to think of it just sitting on a shelf with no one enjoying it."

"But you don't know me," Billy protested. "We've never met before."

"I don't need to know someone long before I decide if I like them or not. You're a good bloke, Bill, I can tell. Look, here's what I'll do. I'll finish my pint and leave the tankard here. You take it if you want, or leave it if you want and someone else can take it. No pressure. It's up to you."

Billy glanced over to the corner table of the bar where Harry, Tommy No-Legs and the man with the dog were sitting. If he had his own tankard hanging up behind the bar, it would really make him someone. None of the rest of them had their own tankard.

"Thanks," he said. "Thanks very much. I will."

"Great!" The stranger beamed again. "You go back and join your friends, and I'll give you a wave when I'm going. I appreciate what you're doing."

The stranger shook Billy's hand and then turned back to the bar and to his pint, his business done. Billy took his pint over to his friends and joined their conversation about the previous evening's football.

After a while, Billy, who had been watching when he could, saw the stranger drain his pint, cast a half-wave in Billy's direction and leave the bar. It coincided almost exactly with Billy finishing his own pint. No one else was at the bar, so he went over, ready to order a fresh pint from Jenny the barmaid and ask to have it in his own tankard. When he got to the bar, however, he saw that the tankard was full, the foam on the beer spilling over the rim and running down the side to make a puddle on the bar top. Jenny was chatting and laughing with a couple of young men at the other end of the bar, so Billy had a sip of his beer, then waited for a minute or so until it looked good, then carried his pint over to his friends.

The rest of the evening passed in something of a blur for Billy—a blur of good conversation, healthy debate, friendship and beer. As he lurched home, he felt light-headed, unsteady on his feet, but good. His new tankard was behind the bar, and try as he might, he could not remember going back for a refill after the first time. He must have done; he could not possibly be feeling like this after just two pints. The only thing that cast doubt into his mind was that he appeared to have more money left in his pocket than he expected. He had ended many nights with less money than he thought; that was something you accepted when you went out for a pint. But as Billy drifted off to sleep and tried to think back to the number of pints he had consumed and how much they must have cost, he could only think that either he had come out with more money than he thought, or that tight bugger Stavros must have put his hand in his pocket for once and bought a couple of rounds.

The next few nights followed the same pattern: Billy went to the King's Head, ordered a pint from Jenny (in his tankard, of course, which now had its own place behind the bar), spent the evening chatting to the other lads, then went home, pleasantly drunk but not much lighter in the pocket. On the fourth night, a Friday, the boys started to ask questions about Billy's tankard.

"That's a pretty nice tankard," Stavros remarked. "Haven't seen it before."

"I've had it a while," Billy replied. "You just haven't noticed. Mind you, you haven't noticed that City are crap either."

The other lads laughed at this. Of them all, Stavros was the only one who supported City. It was, in fact, where he got his nickname. When City signed a striker from a club in Greece for an absurd amount of money a few years earlier, Stavros, who was still called Brian then, went on and on about how this was going to help City win the League. The striker spent most of the season either injured or on the bench and was then sold on for a loss when City failed to win the League or even come close. The striker had long since been forgotten in most places, but not in the King's Head. Bringing City up now, however, proved to be a mistake because Stavros was determined to deflect the laughter away from himself.

"So what is it?" he asked. "Stainless steel?"

"No, it's pewter, I think," Billy replied as casually as he could.

"Oh, pewter, is it?" Stavros roared with fake laughter. "*Pewter*? Glass not good enough for you now?"

"I just like it, that's all."

"Never liked my beer out of metal." Stavros was unwilling to let it go. "Tastes like it comes out of a can."

"Each to his own," Harry intervened. Whenever an argument broke out about anything, it was always Harry who was the peacemaker. "Anyone for another?"

"I'll get these," Billy said quickly, keen to get away from Stavros, who was still eyeing the tankard, and Billy didn't like it. He went to the bar and brought back five pints. It took him two trips, and as he was returning the second time, it occurred to him that Jenny only seemed to have charged him for four. He nearly went back to query it but didn't. When he sat down, the conversation had moved on to a middle-aged man who was sitting over the other side of the bar, and speculation about who the pretty young thing draped all over him might be. The tankard was not mentioned again that night.

Billy's tankard was brought up again the following night by Tommy No-Legs. Quite how Tommy lost his legs had never really been established because the story varied. Sometimes it was an accident at a building site, sometimes a car accident, but they humoured his tales because Tommy was getting on a bit. Billy liked Tommy, though. He was pleasant, good-humoured and always laughed at jokes about him not drinking too much in case he got legless.

"That's an interesting handle on your tankard," Tommy remarked. "Can I have a look?"

Billy reluctantly turned the tankard around so Tommy could get a better look but stopped short of passing it over to his friend.

"Nice," Tommy said. "What is it? Bone or something?"

"No, I think it's plastic." Billy covered the handle with his hand and changed the subject. "Was that a new carer tonight, Tom?"

"Yes. Liz, I think her name is. She's just started. She's bloody useless, but who cares when you're being pushed around by someone who looks like that?"

They laughed at this, and the chat moved on, but all the same, Billy felt uneasy going home that night. First Stavros and now Tommy had taken an interest in the tankard. He hoped it was because it was something new and that jealousy wasn't creeping in.

Billy woke up on Sunday morning with a strange, anxious feeling gnawing at the pit of his stomach. Billy was not generally prone to anxiety. He normally just got on with living his life and had not felt anxious about anything much since those first horrible months after Sheila left. Once he realised he was absolutely fine on his own, he had calmed down and not really worried about anything since. He shook the feeling off and went back to sleep. When he finally got up, just after eleven, he had some breakfast and got on with tidying the house. It was while he was washing some of that week's coffee mugs that the nagging feeling of anxiety returned, and he realised what it was. While he was here washing mugs and hoovering, the other lads would be at the pub ordering their lunchtime drinks, and while they were doing so,

Billy's tankard would be sitting behind the bar. Jenny didn't work on a Sunday; it was another barmaid called Carol, and what if Stavros or maybe Tommy convinced her that the tankard was his? They might find out the incredible things the tankard could do, and once they knew that, they would certainly want it for themselves. Billy couldn't risk that. The tankard was *his*. The stranger had given it to him because he was special. Nobody else was going to get their jealous, thieving hands on it. He abandoned his washing-up, changed from his Sunday scruff into something a bit more appropriate and walked along the canal to the King's Head.

When he got to the pub, Harry, Stavros and Tommy were already present and deep in conversation. The man with the dog wasn't there, but he tended to have Sundays off, too. As Billy drew close, they all looked up in surprise.

"All right, Bill?" Harry said. "You know it's Sunday, don't you?"

Billy was just about to make something up about fancying a change when he stopped short in horror as he saw what Harry was drinking out of.

"That's *my* tankard."

"Oh, yes, sorry," Harry said. "Carol gave it to me by mistake. I was going to pass it back when I'd finished."

"Give it back," Billy said. "It's mine."

"No problem," Harry replied. "I'll just finish this and—"

"*Now.*"

"Take it easy, Billy lad," Tommy said. "Harry didn't mean anything. It was an honest mistake."

"Of course it was," Billy said, his fists clenching with rage. "It looks so much like a glass one, doesn't it?"

"Look, here you go," Harry said, draining the tankard and holding it out to Billy. "No harm done."

Billy snatched the tankard back and went over to the bar. While he was waiting for Carol to serve him, he seethed at the nerve of Harry. No harm? You didn't go around stealing other people's property and then say no harm. He looked down at his tankard and saw that it was now filled with a perfectly pulled pint with a smooth, creamy head on top, even though Carol had still been nowhere near. He thought for one moment about buying Harry a pint to make up for snapping at him but changed his mind. Harry could buy his own pints from now on. He took a sip from what turned out to be the best pint he had tasted in a long time and went back to join the others.

Billy stayed longer than he'd intended, all thoughts of tidying and shopping forgotten. The beer in his tankard tasted so good that he nursed the same pint all afternoon, refusing any offers of another pint from anyone else. He didn't usually drink this slowly, but the ale was so good he was savouring every mouthful. What was even better was that he never seemed to reach the bottom, until somehow, it got to five o'clock and Harry announced that it was time he went home. Billy also decided he had drunk enough. Maybe it was because he wasn't used to drinking on a Sunday, but despite only drinking one pint, he was feeling pleasantly tipsy. When he stood up, his legs felt wobbly and he had to put a hand on the table for support.

"I'll walk along with you," Harry offered. "You're looking a bit unsteady there, mate."

Billy wanted to refuse, but Harry insisted, so Billy tucked his tankard in his coat pocket in case anyone else got any ideas, and together they walked under the bridge and onto the canal towpath.

"Listen, Bill," Harry said, "I'm sorry about using your tankard. Carol just gave it to me and I didn't want to waste a pint."

"No problem," Billy said. He wished Harry hadn't reminded him. He'd almost forgotten about it.

"So what's the deal with it? Is it a trick or something?"

Billy stopped and stared at him.

"What do you mean?"

"Have you got some deal with the pub? When Carol gave it to me, she didn't charge me. I thought it was a mistake."

"Yes, it was," Billy told him carefully, placing a hand on the tankard in his pocket. The cool feel of the metal felt reassuring. "It was a mistake."

"But it happened twice," Harry said and grinned. "It's a great thing. No wonder you won't let anyone else use it."

Billy felt a hot anger rising in him. He had a sudden, uncontrollable desire to wipe the stupid grin off Harry's face, and before he could stop himself, he had lashed out. He only realised that he still had the tankard in his hand when it connected with the side of Harry's head. Harry staggered, a trickle of blood running down his forehead and a shocked look on his face, and then, before Billy could do anything to stop him, toppled sideways into the canal. Billy stood rooted to the spot and watched Harry thrash once, then sink under the water. He stared at the tankard in his hand, at the red smear of blood and the shallow dent on the edge of its base, and at the surface of the canal where the ripples from Harry's fall were spreading wider and wider. Then he somehow managed to get his legs moving and ran home.

Once inside his house, Billy slammed the door shut and locked it. He stood with his back against the door breathing hard and quite unable to decide what to do next. He thought about calling an ambulance or the police, but everyone had seen him and Harry leaving the pub together. He could claim it was an accident and Harry had slipped into the canal, but how would that explain his head wound? What if they wanted to take his tankard in as evidence? He'd never get it back. He double-checked that he'd locked the door securely and went into the living room to sit down.

Outside, the evening was beginning to draw in, but he didn't turn on the light. It was better if nobody thought he was at home. He took his tankard out of his pocket and inspected it. He must have been mistaken when he thought he saw a dent earlier; it looked perfect now. The smear of blood had darkened to a black smudge, which came off when he rubbed a spit-moistened finger over it. The tankard now looked pristine again, and Billy put it down on the coffee table next to his armchair. When he looked at it again, it was filled with beer. *Well*, Billy thought, *a quick one won't hurt.*

He was halfway through the pint when a horrible thought occurred to him; there were houses backing onto that stretch of the canal. He hadn't seen anyone in their garden or peering out of the window, but then he hadn't been looking. What if someone had seen what had happened and called the police? They could be on their way now, and it really wouldn't do if they arrived and found Billy sitting here drinking beer. He gulped the rest of the pint down and put the tankard back on the coffee table. As he did so, beer foam slopped out over the brim and onto the table. The tankard was full again. He snatched it up and drank it in three long swallows. He had not even taken it away from his mouth when he felt the foam tickling his upper lip and knew that the tankard was full again. Halfway through the first pint, he wondered briefly if tipping the beer down the sink would have the same effect, but by now, he was committed. He had to drain it before the police got here, so he continued to drink like a parched man in a desert.

The police entered the house nearly a day later, and only then because one of the neighbours had heard a crash and couldn't get an answer. They found Billy's body before they found Harry's, which would not surface for another two days, when it became entangled in the lines belonging to two youths who were trying their hand at fishing in the canal. Both bodies were soaked, Harry's from the water, Billy's from beer. Billy was found flat on his back in his living room, lying on the pieces of a shattered coffee table and surrounded by a pool of beer and vomit and urine.

The post-mortem showed that his stomach and lungs were filled with beer; put simply, he had drowned in best bitter. The one thing no one was able to explain at the inquest was how he had done it. There were no bottles or cans in the house, and yet he had drunk so much that it would have been impossible for him to stand, let alone walk. The only thing the police had been able to find, nestling amongst the wreckage of the table, was an old, battered, rusty tankard with a broken handle and a large hole in the base, but there was no way anybody could have drunk a drop from that. The tankard was thrown on a skip when the council came to clear the house, along with the rest of Billy King's worldly goods. There was so much junk in the skip that nobody noticed when a well-dressed man wandered past one night, fished the tankard out from under a shabby mattress and strolled away whistling to himself.

DRIVE

TOM MOSS THREW the holdall into the boot of his car and slammed the hatch shut. He had packed in a hurry and had no idea if he had put enough in the holdall or it he had packed the right things. He had just grabbed some clothes out of the drawers in his bedroom and rammed them into the bag. He didn't have the time or the inclination to check what was there or fold them. That had been Nicola's domain. She was the one who made the lists and laid everything out on the bed in the spare room, checking off her list with everything she folded and stacked. She was the one who knew exactly how much would fit in each bag and the best way to pack it, but she wouldn't ever be doing it again, so his way would just have to do. If he needed anything else, he could buy it. Sometimes when you had to go, you just had to do it. He got into the car, scratching absently at the scab on the back of his hand from a cut he had picked up somewhere, started the engine and drove off.

He had gone no more than half a mile when it occurred to him to check he had enough petrol to get him where he was going, and it was as well he did: a glance at the gauge told him he didn't even have enough in the tank to get him out of Liverpool. He stopped at the petrol station along Derby Road, filled up and bought a packet of overpriced cigarettes, handing over his credit card and hoping to God there was enough on it. He was going to need what cash he had for the Tunnel and to buy some food when he reached the cottage. After that, he would have to wait a week or so until payday, which was going to have to do him for some time, seeing as it might be his last. He tore the cellophane off the cigarette packet and pulled one out, lighting it with one of the throwaway lighters he always kept in his jacket pocket, and accelerated out of the petrol station. He kept to the speed limit so as not to draw attention to himself, all the while wishing the miles would pass more quickly. He wanted to be through the Tunnel and away from Liverpool as soon as possible.

As he passed Merseyside Police Headquarters, he kept his eyes fixed on the road ahead. If he had his way, he would never set foot inside the building again, and he was very much aware people in there who would be wondering where he was and why he hadn't shown up for work that morning. They would have to wonder. Maybe Craig Devaney or Anjil Desai on his team might have an idea about what was going on, but he trusted them not to get involved in any speculation. Anjil had been at his side the day the Albert Dock gave up its dead and would shut down any rumour mongering. He had been working with Craig up until the day before, too, and knew he had an ally there. By the time anyone found that the files he had shoved in the bottom of his holdall were gone, he would also be gone.

As he passed through the darkness of the Queensway Tunnel, he was increasingly aware of the flashing light on his phone, which he had tossed onto the passenger seat. He didn't know how many messages and calls he had missed and didn't want to know. At the deepest part of the Tunnel, and with a large builders' van behind him, he snatched the phone off the seat, opened his window halfway and dropped the phone out. By the time anyone found it, they would have to scoop it up with a shovel. Now that nobody could contact him, he felt better immediately. He had many miles to go before he could think about relaxing but it was a start. He wondered briefly how many of the calls he had missed were from work, and whether any of them had been from Nicola. He doubted she had called. Since the day she had left, she'd only ever contacted him through her friend Becca, with whom Moss was still on reasonably good terms, or more usually through her solicitor. He didn't blame her; he couldn't live with himself, so there was no possibility anyone else could live with him. It wasn't his fault either. The blame lay squarely with the girl in the dock, or more accurately with whatever bastard had put her there. Moss and Nicola's marriage was just another victim.

***

Moss could never quite understand why, after more than twenty years' service and more crime scenes than he cared to count, the death of one young woman should have affected him so deeply. He didn't know her—apparently, nobody did since she had yet to be identified—and couldn't even say he had a daughter that age or anything like that. She was just another anonymous corpse that nobody loved enough to claim, and Moss had seen plenty of those before, the lost, the homeless, the vagrants, people who had lost everything and finally their lives in a city that feigned shock at the statistics but was ultimately too busy to care. He'd attended the scene when one man had been found in an alley and had been lying behind the bins for so long that his clothes had become fused to the filth beneath him, so that it looked for all the world as though he were growing out of the ground. He'd been there when another homeless, nameless man had died as paramedics tried to revive him after he had been kicked multiple times by a gang of kids who had filmed it on their phones for fun. Yet when he'd been called to the Albert Dock one icy December morning, it had started Moss on a path that would finish his marriage and quite possibly his career and all because the dead girl wouldn't go away.

It was two weeks before Christmas. All the shops, restaurants and bars around the dock had their decorations and lights up. Business had been brisk the previous night, and most people had been too busy enjoying themselves, or too drunk to notice the body in the water. Even if they had seen it, they could be forgiven for thinking they were looking at some discarded clothes. All that was visible was the back of a jacket, which had billowed above the surface and then frozen solid on one of the rare nights cold enough for it to do so. A man named Damien Lennon (no relation, but everyone asked) had spotted it. He had been out with friends and they'd gone back to one of their number's waterfront apartment. As the sober, designated driver, he had become bored with their antics, which got progressively louder as the evening wore on, and had gone out to get some air. He had been so enthralled by the view of the dock and the eerie way the moonlight reflected off the ice that, even though it was four in the morning, he had started to take photographs on his phone.

At first, he'd thought what he was seeing was the usual flotsam that gathered on the surface of the water, but the more he looked, the more concerned he became that perhaps he was seeing something else. He went as close to the edge of the dock as he dared, aware that the brickwork was sparkling with frost and one false move could send him to join whatever was in the water. He tried to use the torch on his phone to see better, but it didn't help. He could only think of one thing to do, and that was to call the police. If it was a body floating there, then an ambulance likely wouldn't be much use. He texted his friends to let them know where he was, and waited.

Two uniformed officers arrived around half an hour later, and as soon as they had established that it was, indeed, a body, Detective Inspector Tom Moss, who was only an hour and a half away from going home after a long shift, took the call to come out. If the body had not been discovered until the morning, things would have turned out very differently for Moss.

There were two things he would never forget from that night. The first was the noise the body made when the police divers pulled it away from the ice. There was a crack and a tearing sound like someone ripping Velcro apart, and then a peculiar gurgle as water seeped up through the hole the body had made. It was one of the strangest things Moss had ever heard, and he was never quite sure why, but the thing that would haunt him for many nights to come was the appearance of the body itself. He had seen bodies fished out of the water before and knew that he could expect it to be bloated and fish-bitten, but when the body was laid on the dock wall and then turned over, he hadn't anticipated that it would have no face at all. It would later be established that the girl's face had been viciously smashed in by whoever had killed her (by strangulation, it turned out) and her fingertips burned off, presumably to prevent identification. At that moment, however, it had looked for all the world to Moss as though the face had been left behind when the body was torn from the ice, and he thought that if he were to look over the dock wall, he would see a face on the ice, inverted like the back of a mask. He didn't look.

The girl carried no identification, and the thorough demolition job that had been done on her made putting a name to the body almost impossible. The usual checks on scars (several), tattoos (none) and broken bones (left wrist, many years prior) gave up no useful information, and Moss and his team could only put out the vaguest appeals for help in the media, which unsurprisingly elicited no response. Like so many others, the girl was destined to be buried in an unmarked grave, missed and mourned by no one. But Moss was unable to let it go.

***

He emerged from the Tunnel, threw his toll money into the basket and took the slip road onto the motorway that would take him across the Wirral and out towards North Wales. He wasn't quite sure where the idea to go to Anglesey had come from. He had many childhood memories of family holidays there, roaming around the beaches and clifftops, hunting through rock pools, fascinated by the worlds of life he found there. They were carefree times, years before heart attacks robbed him of both his parents and before an ugly world had turned him cynical. He supposed that Anglesey represented a happier, safer time in his life, when he was surrounded by the love of his parents and had no worries about bills or murders or wives who would walk out one day and not look back. He had a desperate need to get back to that life, and when he had woken up that morning, he could think of little else. He had to go, and go now, so he did. He didn't feel as though he were running away from his problems; rather, he was running towards something better. Perhaps he would be able to stop there and breathe and think, and maybe, just maybe, come up with some answers to the questions that had been filling his head for months.

He tried to push all other thoughts out and concentrate on the traffic and the road ahead, but he was tired through stress and lack of sleep and would soon need some caffeine to keep him awake. Just past Flint, he saw a sign for a service station and pulled off the dual carriageway and into the car park, stopping alongside a white van with a red logo on the side advertising 'Saunders Solutions'. *Solutions to what?* Probably nothing he needed. He unbuckled his seat belt, wound down the window and lit a cigarette, smoking it in long, slow drags. When it was down to its stub and he felt a bit more like facing people, he wound the window back up, got out of the car and dropped the cigarette end on the floor, grinding it out under his heel.

He took a deep breath and went into the service station coffee shop, glad it was one that belonged to a big chain, as whoever served him would stick to the usual corporate script and wouldn't try making conversation. He ordered the largest black coffee they did and took it to a table near the window, from where he could see his car outside. Years of police work had trained him always to get a window seat where he could; sometimes it was useful to watch the world outside or see who was coming in. He didn't anticipate that anyone would have followed him, but you never knew and it was best to be safe. He took the lid off his coffee and waited for a moment before drinking; he had scalded his lips on too many takeaway coffees, another occupational hazard.

It was while he was waiting for his coffee to be drinkable that he noticed the girl. She was sitting at a table on her own, and his copper's instinct told him straight away that there was something wrong. She looked to be in her late teens, maybe early twenties. She had long, straight hair from which the blonde dye had almost faded, on top of that a woollen hat, pulled down almost to her eyebrows. Her face was pale and might have been pretty, but she looked tired and drawn. The policeman in him noticed two things missing from the table in front of her. She had no drink, for a start, which would probably get her moved on if any of the staff spotted it, but it was the other thing that was missing that was ringing alarm bells. Moss had seen plenty of kids her age sitting in cafés and bars, and the first thing they did was put their phones on the table so that whatever happened, they could monitor their online social lives. This girl had no phone. Moss tried to take his eyes off her and concentrate on his coffee, but he couldn't. It was the hair. She had the kind of hair that had plagued his sleeping and waking life for months.

Maybe it was because he'd only known what the girl from the dock looked like from behind. He would never know her face. The description his team had been able to give the press was that she was female, late teens/early twenties, with long, straight, brown hair that had been dyed blonde until recently when she seemed to have been growing it out. He soon found out how useless a description that was; girls like that were everywhere. Time and time again, he would see one in the street, on their own or with a partner or a group of friends. If he could, he would start to follow them, hoping they would turn so that he could see their faces, not knowing what he hoped to gain by doing so. They weren't the girl from the dock, couldn't be, and could offer no clue, but a part of his brain wanted reassurance that they had faces.

The ones he saw while he was awake all did; it was the ones he saw in his dreams that tormented him. The dreams often followed the same path as real life, and he would be walking down the street following a girl with long, straight hair. Then she would turn, and there would be a mess of flesh and muscle and bone where her face should be, and Moss would wake up sweating and sometimes crying, and stay awake, fearful of going back to sleep and seeing it again. It wasn't long before Nicola started to complain that he was disturbing her sleep, and to keep the peace he moved into the spare room. It was only after one late night at the Police Club, celebrating another lucky bastard's retirement that Moss collapsed, drunk, into his bed and slept through without dreaming. After that, he tried to go to bed drunk every night. If he couldn't go to bed drunk, he would dream and then sneak downstairs to have a drink or two so that he wouldn't dream anymore when he went back.

It was on one of these nights that he ended his marriage. He was sitting in the living room with a tumbler of Jack Daniel's in his hand and the lights off when Nicola came downstairs for a glass of water. When she saw him sitting there, it startled her so much that she dropped the glass.

"Jesus, Tom! What are you doing? Are you drinking? It's three o'clock!"

"I need to sleep."

"Then go to bed and sleep. Don't just sit here getting pissed."

"I have to. I'll see her if I don't."

"Those bloody dreams! Tom, she's dead, and you're not going to find out who she was. You've got to accept that. Honest to God, I don't know how much more of this I can take."

Moss drained his glass and looked at her through bleary eyes. "How do you think I feel?"

"Then let it go. Get some help if you need it, but let it go. She was just some homeless druggie. It's not like you knew her." Nicola stopped there, and her eyes widened with sudden realisation. "You didn't, did you? Oh God, Tom, did you know her? Don't tell me you were screwing her, too!"

Moss would barely remember doing it later, but before he could stop himself, he was on his feet with his hand drawn back. The slap was the loudest thing in that house for the next two days. Any time Moss and Nicola spent together was passed in silence. She would not speak to him and he couldn't speak to her; all he could see was the red mark on her face, which her make-up hardly concealed, and all he could think of was that this was how destroying someone's face started. On the third day, Moss came home from work to find Nicola gone.

His marriage ended that night, but the dreams and the drinking didn't. He tried to get on with his job, hoping nobody would notice—he had always been good at hiding a hangover—but Craig and especially Anjil were asking him more and more frequently if he was okay, and he knew he wouldn't be able to hide it much longer. He didn't much like some of the other questions Craig was asking either. He needed to get away and be somewhere where he could deal with it all with no one watching.

***

The girl got up from her seat and left the coffee shop. Moss stared down at his cup so he wouldn't have to see her from behind. When he looked up again, she was standing outside, near his car, talking to a man who was leaning against the open door of the Saunders Solutions van. She asked him something and pointed, and he shook his head. Then he got into the van and drove off. Moss left half of his coffee and went out to the car park. She was still standing there, where Mr. Saunders Solutions had left her, looking downcast and lost.

"You okay?" he asked, making a show of getting out his car keys.

"Yeah, fine," she said in a quiet voice betraying an accent from somewhere in the Midlands, maybe Birmingham. "Just needed a lift. He wasn't going my way."

"Where are you heading?"

"Bangor."

"Student?"

She nodded.

"I'm headed for Anglesey. I can drop you if you want."

The girl hesitated, but Moss reached into his pocket and took out his warrant card wallet, flashing her the badge.

"It's okay," he said. "I'm police."

He got into his car and opened the passenger door. She paused briefly, then glanced around and got in. As soon as she did so, Moss regretted it. The last thing he wanted was a passenger, but from somewhere, the old, responsible Tom Moss had surfaced and couldn't see a girl like that hanging around a service station car park where she could accept a lift off just about anybody.

"I'm Tom," he said as she fastened her seat belt.

She smiled briefly but didn't reply. It was probably best not to know her name. Just drop her off and get on.

"Haven't you got a bag or anything?"

"No."

He pulled out of the car park and re-joined the dual carriageway. They drove on in silence for a while, Moss not looking at her, just at the road. She was nobody, a skint student hitching back to uni. He didn't want to know her name, didn't want to know her story, and didn't want to get involved. He wanted to see her safely to Bangor and forget her. He had made the mistake of getting involved before and wasn't going there again.

***

Her name was Amy, and Moss should have left her alone. She was a homeless, recovering drug addict, and Moss had met her when she had been caught up in a street fight. The fight was nothing to do with her; she had been trying to stop it but had received a punch in the face for her trouble. Moss wasn't sure why he took to her so much. She had a pleasant, open personality and was positive and good-humoured despite her troubles and a rapidly swelling lip. He kept a check on her over the following weeks, to make sure she was okay. He shouldn't have given her his phone number, and he certainly shouldn't have slept with her. Nicola found out because Amy kept texting him, wouldn't leave him alone. There followed rows, recriminations and eventually an uneasy forgiveness. Moss severed all connections with Amy, of course, and by the time a year had passed, Nicola had stopped mentioning it.

The night Moss hit her was the first time she had brought it up in a very long time, and it had touched a nerve. Even if she said she had forgiven him, he had never forgiven himself and had lashed out to shut her up. Moss's indiscretion had failed to wreck his marriage the first time but had succeeded the second, and he vowed when he deleted Amy's number from his phone that he would never get involved with anyone like that again. He had nearly managed it.

***

The girl was looking out of the window and Moss was trying hard not to look at the back of her head. A road sign told him that he was twenty-six miles from Bangor. If the traffic stayed like this, he would be free of her in less than an hour. Ten miles or so back, Moss had turned on the radio to break the silence, and when he heard the voice, he thought at first it was someone on the radio. But then she spoke again, her voice muffled by the fact that she was speaking into the glass.

"Why are you running?" she asked.

"What? I'm not. I'm just…going away."

"You're running. But you can't. It goes with you."

"I don't know what you're talking about."

"What you did. It goes with you. You can pretend you've forgotten, but you haven't. Not really."

"Look, I don't know what you've been taking—"

"You drank to forget, but it's still there."

Moss gripped the steering wheel tighter, his knuckles white. There was something there, behind the fog in his mind, something he didn't want to see.

"I think you should shut up," he said. "You don't know me. You don't know a thing—"

"I know you," the girl said. "I know you killed me."

Then she turned her head and he saw it. He saw what was left of her face after he had battered it over and over again. He could feel the scrape of one of her teeth as it broke off and scratched the back of his hand. He saw the ruin he had left behind because this time Nicola couldn't find out, the sight he had tried to obliterate from his mind and so nearly had.

"Remember me?" she said, and he screamed.

***

They identified him by his warrant card badge. There was not much else to identify him with. When the car swerved across two lanes of the dual carriageway and hit a lorry head on, he'd gone through the windscreen, and the glass had torn his face to shreds. The North Wales Police officers who attended the scene commented that a copper really should have been obeying the law and wearing his seat belt. No one could explain why he'd lost control of the car; maybe he'd fallen asleep at the wheel, or he was still drunk from the night before. There was certainly enough alcohol in his system. The one thing everyone agreed, though, was that it was a miracle nobody else was injured in the crash. Even the lorry driver escaped unscathed. It was, they said, just as well there was no one else in the car at the time.

SCUT'S REVENGE

OBITUARY

Edward James 'Eddie' Agnew
14th November 1950 – 10th February 2017

Eddie Agnew, the prolific author of children's fiction, has passed away peacefully at home, aged 67, his literary agent confirmed today.

Agnew was the author of twenty-seven best-selling books featuring his world-famous creation *Scut the Scruffy Bunny*. The stories tell of the adventures of Scut, a cuddly toy rabbit who was 'a little bit loose at the seams through years of love', and the other loveable toy characters who come to life after their owner has gone to bed.

Trained as a journalist, Agnew had two thrillers published in the late 1970s. They were published through a small-press imprint and received little or no critical attention. It was only when his first children's book, *Scut the Scruffy Bunny*, was published in 1983 that he became a household name. The first book was famously written in response to the demands of his beloved son, Mark, for a new bedtime story, and this tale was populated with Mark's own toys. The most recent book in the series, *Scut Needs a Stitch*, was published in 2016 and, like all the books that preceded it, became an instant bestseller.

That was just the opening to the obituary in *The Guardian* for Eddie Agnew. It went on for another eight sycophantic paragraphs and regurgitated the stories everybody knew. All the other papers ran similar stories, all of them wrong. Eddie Agnew was not sixty-seven. His son Mark was not 'beloved'. The toy on which Scut was based did not belong to Mark, and the first book was not written in response to Mark asking for a bedtime story. But the biggest lie in this fiction was that although Eddie Agnew did indeed die at home, his death was anything but peaceful. I know the truth about Eddie's life because my name is Mark Agnew, and I am his supposedly 'beloved' son. I know the truth about his death because it was me who found him.

Eddie Agnew was, in fact, born in 1945, a good five years before the date given in his official biographies. He started lying about his age when *Scut the Scruffy Bunny* was published in 1983. For some reason, he believed that thirty-three was a better age to start a career in children's fiction than thirty-eight. It would not really have made any difference. Thanks in part to the sensitive and touching illustrations provided by Helena Holland, the book became first a word-of-mouth, then a domestic success and finally a global phenomenon. If Eddie's age was deemed to be relevant in his earliest interviews, it was never mentioned again. The books would have sold in their millions, whatever his age was supposed to be.

Age was by no means the only untruth in the legend of Eddie Agnew. The idea that Scut was created to tell me a bedtime story was nonsense. My father never told me a story in his life. That sort of thing was left to my mother until the day she decided she could not tolerate Eddie anymore and left. After that I was largely ignored. Scut was not based on any of my toys, either. I didn't really have any. My father once told me he saw the rabbit in a charity shop and quite liked it, even though he didn't like it enough to buy it for me. In truth, the first Scut book was the product of a drunken bet Eddie made with one of his disreputable friends. They had apparently been discussing Eddie's lack of publishing success, and Eddie had been raging about the attention children's authors received. He bet his friend that he could get a children's book published, and his friend accepted the bet. He spotted the rabbit in the charity shop and wrote the first book in less than an hour.

While we're debunking myths, we need to consider the role Helena Holland played in my father's legend. Her illustration of the Scut books has received well-deserved credit for the contribution it made to my father's success. When you think of Scut, you think of Holland's coloured pencil drawings and their almost dream-like quality. The toys of Scut and his friends bear Holland's designs and colours, and even the short-lived cartoon series in the 1990s was very distinctly Helena Holland. My father's funeral was not well attended, but Helena was there, a small, forlorn figure sitting at the back. I have heard that her livelihood is going to survive my father's passing. Apart from the continued royalties, she has genuine talent and will never be short of offers of work. I'm very pleased for Helena; she is a lovely lady and has never told how she came to illustrate the books or the truth about her working relationship with my father.

She has never told, for example how she came to meet him. Everyone knows that Helena was a penniless artist who happened to be sitting in a café sketching passers-by when who should walk in but Eddie Agnew. Myth loves coincidence, so of course, that would be just after Eddie had tried to pitch his children's story to an agent, only to be told by the agent that while it was a nice story, he 'just couldn't visualise it'. Eddie happened to see Helena's sketches, bought her a coffee, described his book and changed both their lives. With some freshly drawn pictures of Scut to support the story, Eddie and his new friend raced back to the agent, who famously looked at the pictures and said,

"Now I see it!" It's an incredible rags-to-riches story, but a story is all it is, one dreamed up by said agent, Gordon Kent, to capture the imagination of an audience ahead of the launch of the first Scut book and almost entirely untrue.

Ellen Holland (the 'Helena' came later) was an unknown artist, but she was already on Gordon Kent's books when Eddie brought his story in. It is true that Kent felt he could not visualise the characters in Eddie's book, but he spent several days going through the work of the artists he represented until he found the one whose style he thought best suited Eddie's words. That artist didn't want the job, but Kent struck lucky with his second choice, and, after a quick alteration to the artist's name, the team of Agnew and Holland was born.

I have never been sure why Helena continued to work with my father for so long. It was not for want of money or work, that is certain, because the Scut books brought her plenty of both. She may very well have cared about what she was doing and the service she was providing to generations of adoring children. It certainly was not because she liked my father. He bullied her as he did anybody who had the misfortune to have any dealings with him. I remember one occasion, when I was about eleven, while my father and Helena were working on what would be the fifth of the Scut books. My father was in his study, a room that was his private and personal domain, and I heard him shout. I thought he had called me and came running because it simply was not done to ignore Eddie when he called. I stopped outside the study door, however, when I realised that he was not calling for me but shouting at someone on the telephone.

"I don't care if you *are* busy, you stupid woman! I need to start seeing some pictures, and I need to see them now!"

I sat at the foot of the stairs, not wanting to intrude but somehow unable to move.

"Then make some fucking time!" he hollered. "There are plenty of other artists who would be glad of the work!"

At the crash of the phone being slammed down, I ran upstairs as quietly as I could in case he caught me and thought I was eavesdropping, though in truth his voice could be heard all around the house when he was in a temper.

But Helena carried on working with him until the end. I suppose the increase in the use of email made it easier to deal with him from a distance, though God knows what his emails must have looked like. I have no desire to check. His computer has not been switched on since the day he died, and I have no intention of changing that. Gordon Kent asked me to look to see if there was any unfinished work on it, but as far as I'm concerned, it would be better if Scut the Scruffy Bunny died the day my father did.

In fact, there were many occasions when I am sure Eddie would have preferred it if his creation had predeceased him. The truth, which was only ever known to my mother, while she was still around, and me, was that Eddie Agnew despised Scut and every book in which he appeared. He carried on writing them for the money they brought in, which he enjoyed to the full but never forgave that poor rabbit for, as he thought it, depriving him of the chance to be a proper writer. Even when Gordon Kent reluctantly tried to have Eddie's two earlier thrillers reissued, no publishing house would touch them. Eddie Agnew writing *Scut the Scruffy Bunny* was the golden goose, but no one would conceive of him writing anything else.

It was this hatred of his creation that led to the production of the small pamphlets Eddie wrote, illustrated in a crude parody of Helena's style and distributed to what few friends he had. The first, *Scut Comes to Dinner*, had the unfortunate rabbit accidentally falling into a pan of boiling water and ending up on the menu. Subsequent tales saw Scut meeting his demise in a variety of increasingly sick ways or engaging in semi-pornographic encounters with some of the other characters from the books. It is my belief that it was these slim volumes and their contents that led to Scut hating Eddie back.

There is one other character in this tale that I have not yet introduced—if you can call a stuffed toy animal a character. When the books were at the height of their popularity, an enterprising toy company marketed a very successful range of replicas of Scut and his pals. They all sold well, but Scut himself and White-Ear, the object of Scut's innocent affections, were the most popular. White-Ear, with her distinctive one white ear was, of course, also a star of some of Eddie's less salubrious parodies. When the range of toys was produced, Eddie was sent one of each of the toys, most of which he kept in a box in his office, still in their cellophane wrappers. I can only assume he hoped they would accumulate in value over the years. But there was one he kept out of its wrapper. He kept Scut on a shelf by his desk. That stuffed rabbit sat there and observed Eddie writing his adventures.

There was no way Eddie could ever have sold this particular version of Scut. If the Scut of the stories was a scruffy bunny, this one was just ruined. Its stitching was coming away in several places, leaking stuffing. It was threadbare and its fur was filthy. It was in this condition because Eddie took great delight in hurling it across the room, kicking it and punching it. All of his frustrations at his failure to become a 'real' author were taken out on this toy rabbit, and it showed. Rarely had even the most spiteful child treated a toy so abominably. It is, then, probably quite ironic that it was this very toy that was responsible for Eddie's death.

It was Helena who alerted me to the possibility that something was wrong. She had been trying to get hold of Eddie for a few days by phone and email, so that he could approve some of her latest pictures. When she received no reply, she called at his house. Failing to raise any response from him, she called me.

I still had a key to my father's house, though I never used it. I rarely spoke to him after a series of increasingly bitter rows when I got married. My wife and I had struggled financially through the first years of our marriage, and my father's refusal to give us even a small amount of help led to an estrangement that lasted even after things had begun to improve for us. My wife wanted nothing to do with him, even refusing to take the Agnew name, and neither did I. I kept in touch with Helena, though, and still had the key.

At first, I dismissed Helena's concerns. It was not unheard of for Eddie to take himself off somewhere without telling anyone. But she argued that he had been pestering her for these illustrations, and she was convinced he would not just disappear while he was waiting for them. So reluctantly, I went to his house to investigate. I knocked on the door, and when there was no answer, I let myself in. The first thing I noticed was what appeared to be several days' worth of untouched mail on the mat inside the door. I picked it up and put it on a table in the hall.

At this stage, I was more convinced than ever that I was right about Eddie's whereabouts and Helena was wrong. I stood in the hall listening for any sign of life. Invading Eddie's privacy without warning would almost certainly cause him to fly into a rage, and I was in no mood for an argument. As I listened, I heard a sound coming from somewhere in the house. I couldn't identify what it was or where it was coming from, but it seemed vaguely familiar. I held my breath, and the noise came again, a quiet scraping, like claws on wood. Then I remembered where I had heard it before.

Many years earlier, when I was maybe ten or eleven, there had been an infestation of mice. We only saw one, scampering across the hall and away, but when the house was quiet, scuffling and scratching noises could sometimes be heard behind the skirting boards or in the roof. I think Eddie probably put poison down—he was certainly too mean to get someone in—and after a while, the noises stopped and we forgot about it. It would not have surprised me in the slightest if the mice had returned. On my rare visits to see my father, it was very clear that he had quite low standards of cleanliness and hygiene. There were usually dishes piled in the sink and food debris on the work surfaces. That and the untamed undergrowth of the garden at the back made the house a perfect breeding ground for vermin.

I found the sound disquieting and was on the verge of walking out right there and then. It certainly seemed as though the mice were the only ones home. But just in case, I called out his name ('Eddie', not 'Dad' or 'Father'—I never called him either of those) and listened for a reply. When this was greeted with silence, I was tempted once again to turn around and go home, but something made me go upstairs to his office, to make sure that he was definitely out. It was there that I found him.

I didn't see him immediately. The office door was ajar, but I could not hear any sound from within. I almost knocked on the door but instead pushed it open and peered in. At first, there seemed to be no one around, but something made me go further into the room. It was the flies that alerted me to the fact that something was wrong. Even by my father's lax standards, there were too many of them, zigzagging through the air and crawling across the window and the papers on the desk, their fat, black bodies punctuating the typed text. I cautiously moved to the desk, my heart hammering in anticipation of what I might find. He was lying on his back on the floor behind the desk. His eyes were open and, in my untrained opinion, he had been dead several days or even longer. It was not the open eyes that disturbed me the most, however, or the flies clustering around his nostrils; it was the fact that somehow, impossibly, the head of the stuffed replica of Scut had been forced into his mouth. It looked for all the world as though the rabbit had tried to climb in.

I stood and stared. I could not take in what I was seeing. None of it made sense. Who could possibly have done such a thing? I'm not sure why I neglected to call the police at this point. The obvious conclusion was that Eddie had been murdered, asphyxiated with a soft toy. While there were plenty of people who hated him, the most likely candidates would have been me (because of my history with him and because I had a key) or Helena (because she had called round earlier). Maybe that was why I carefully removed Scut from my father's mouth and put him in my pocket. It may also have been why I checked his mouth for any traces of soft toy stuffing that might have become lodged in his teeth and then gently closed his eyes. It was certainly why I inspected the room for any sign of an intruder before I called the emergency services.

The official cause of Eddie's death was given as cardiac arrest, and his medical records showed that he had been suffering from angina for several years. Eddie left no will, and as he had divorced my mother many years earlier, I have inherited my father's estate. My wife and I will never have to struggle again. I keep the tattered, abused replica of Scut on a shelf in my own office these days. While I am doing my accounts, I exchange conspiratorial glances with him from time to time. The truth about how Eddie Agnew died will never be known to anyone but Scut and me, and he is not saying anything. I am only writing this down because I wonder sometimes what really happened. I wonder if Helena had finally had enough of Eddie's bullying, or if, as I believe can happen, I did something in a fugue state and simply cannot remember. But what bothers me most is that occasionally I catch a glimpse of something in Scut's plastic eye, and a shiver goes through me. He watches me looking after Eddie's estate and making sure all the right decisions are made about Scut and his stories. Every day, I check that he is still in the same position on the shelf. He hasn't moved yet.

THE SNAIL
TERMINATOR

GAVIN WARBURTON'S WIFE, Anthea, often thought he loved his garden nearly as much as he loved her. She was almost right. Although he would never say so because he knew it wouldn't get a warm response, if he were honest, he loved his garden more than he loved Anthea. He loved it so much that when it was threatened, he resorted to desperate measures.

Gavin hadn't always liked gardening. Their previous house only had a paved yard, and even though he tried, at Anthea's request, to liven it up with pots and hanging baskets, it wasn't really a garden. He liked to sit out there in fine weather with a cup of tea or even a glass of wine, but apart from the occasional bit of watering, he had little interest in what grew or didn't grow there. It was only when he retired from the accountancy firm where he had given thirty years of his life and he and Anthea moved to the bungalow that Gavin discovered he had green fingers and liked it.

His father had been a keen gardener. Harry Warburton had not only tended the rose beds and rockeries of his own garden, but he also rented a small allotment from the council. When he was young, Gavin helped his father in the garden or at the allotment by weeding or dead-heading (as Harry directed), pottering around with his own small set of tools and wheelbarrow. Even then, he did it more for the companionship it brought with Harry than because he was interested in learning what the plants were called or when they should be planted or in what conditions. Harry was a taciturn man, and it was only during the time he spent with Gavin in the garden that he took much notice of his son at all. At home, Harry usually had his head buried in the newspaper or his attention fixed on the cricket on the television. It was Gavin's mum who tried to help him with his homework and wanted to know about his day at school, and although Harry still showed no interest in such matters when he and Gavin were gardening together, at least there was some kind of conversation.

Ironically, it was through gardening that Gavin met Anthea, albeit in a roundabout way. She was working in the tea room of a garden centre, the owners of which had got themselves into a bit of a mess with their accounts when the accountant they had been using vanished. He had only vanished as far as Portugal, but nobody knew that at the time. The owners had picked the name of another accountancy firm at random out of the phone book, and that firm, Estevez and Vardy, had sent one of their rising young accountants to go and have a look. That accountant was Gavin Warburton.

Gavin spent the morning with the owners, starting to disentangle the chaos the absconding accountant had left behind, and when they broke for lunch, he availed himself of the centre's tea room. He was served by an attractive, auburn-haired waitress, who, according to her name badge, was called Anthea. Gavin went to the tea room every day for his lunch after that and coincidentally found that the work there was going to take rather longer than he had initially thought. On his last day, once he'd managed to get the garden centre back on track, he called into the tea room one last time. Instead of buying a sandwich and a cup of tea, he asked Anthea if she would like to go to the cinema with him. She surprised him by saying yes. Within a year they were married.

By the time Gavin had been at the accountancy firm (which was now called Estevez Warburton, as he had been made a partner twelve years earlier when Jerry Vardy finally retired) long enough to consider retirement himself, he and Anthea had been married for twenty-eight years. They had brought into the world two daughters, Lucy and Rose, who had grown up, gone to university and were now living miles away. The house where the family had happily resided was now too big for two, and Gavin and Anthea sold it and bought themselves a bungalow in a nicer part of town.

Anthea had been attracted to the bungalow the first time they viewed it, and the garden was one of the things she liked most. Gavin's reaction to both the house and the garden was rather more tepid, largely because he suspected that Anthea would be unwilling to pay for a gardener, and the list of people likely to fulfil that role was a very short list indeed. But, as was usually the way, Anthea got her wish and they moved in.

Gavin's sudden interest in the garden arose out of a combination of two things. One was the fact that spring was pleasantly warm; the other was that until he retired, Gavin had no idea just how many truly awful game shows Anthea watched on the television. They started as soon as she got up and carried on all day, one group of imbeciles after another, each giving progressively worse answers to the most mundane questions. After a few days of shouting "Africa's a continent not a country!" and "It doesn't matter if it was before you were born—don't you read?" Gavin could stand it no longer and retreated outside to look at the garden. And so it began.

It started with a bit of light weeding, to tidy up the existing garden, but once he started, Gavin began to enjoy being outside and away from the banality blaring from the television. As he weeded, he began to see the garden in a whole new light and to imagine its potential. One bed in particular caught his eye. It was currently filled with a random assortment of bedding plants, as if the previous owners had bought a lot of trays, probably on special offer, and planted them with no thought or planning, just to fill the space. Gavin could easily envisage that if the lobelia, alyssum and occasional begonia were to be removed, the bed might be suitable for a vegetable patch. If the garden were to be taken seriously, however, there was one thing he was going to need before anything else; he would need a shed. A ramshackle old greenhouse stood in one corner of the garden and served no practical purpose: Gavin knew straight away this would make an ideal location for the shed. The next day, while Anthea vegetated in front of her shows, he got in the car and went shopping.

Within a week, the shed had been delivered and assembled (by two men from the Shed Centre, not by Gavin), and its proud new owner was able to stand inside it and decide where everything was going to go. The shed Gavin had chosen was big enough to accommodate all his tools and still leave ample space for a comfortable chair and a small workbench. It surely wouldn't be too difficult for a decent electrician to run a cable from the house to the shed and install a double socket. That way, Gavin could have a kettle in his shed and maybe a radio so that he could listen to music and keep up with the news while he worked. It was all taking shape very well indeed.

It took most of the rest of the year for Gavin to get the garden (and indeed the shed) to somewhere near where he wanted. In truth, it all took rather longer than it needed to because he spent more and more time inside the shed, sitting in his chair with the radio on, thinking and planning and not, as he explained to Anthea on the rare occasions when she came to see where he was, napping. He worked hard through the winter, clearing the bed he had earmarked for his vegetable patch, and once he was as sure as he could be that there would be no more frost, he planted seeds and delighted in the green shoots that emerged from the earth with the promise of lettuce and carrots and potatoes. Unfortunately, those green shoots also brought the snails.

Gavin lost an entire crop of lettuce before he even realised what was happening. He got up one morning, and when he went outside with his first cup of tea and inspected his vegetable plot, he saw to his horror that where there had been two neat rows of young lettuce, there was nothing, just bare soil and the occasional stripped stem. His first thought was that he had done something wrong, that maybe his lack of expertise was showing, so he bought another packet of seeds and planted them, checking and double-checking the instructions on the packet. This time, when they began to grow, he caught the culprit.

It was one of those spring days when it had been raining for much of the day but had stayed warm. By the evening, the rain had cleared and the air was damp and humid. Gavin took the cup of tea he always had after his evening meal and went to sit outside. By now, he had two chairs on a paved area in the middle of the garden; the chair intended for Anthea was rarely used, but Gavin got a great deal of use out of his. He loved to sit out and admire his work, occasionally clapping his hands if sparrows took too close an interest in his seeds, or even jumping to his feet, waving his arms like a madman if any of the neighbouring cats dared to set paw in the garden.

On this particular evening, he was sitting with his cup of tea and enjoying the non-game-show silence when he became aware of a noise he had not heard before. It was a quiet but very definite chomping. His first, horrified thought was *rat*, but he had never seen a rat in the garden, despite there being an alleyway at the back, which was often full of rubbish. But when he looked in the direction of the noise, what he saw was probably even more shocking than a rat. On the vegetable bed, working their way slowly and methodically through the young lettuces, were three large snails.

Gavin watched with morbid fascination as the snails slithered over each plant and devoured it, leaving nothing behind. Before they could get much further, he grabbed one by the shell and picked it up. It was only then that he realised he had no idea what to do with it. He stood there holding it at arm's length for a moment and then threw it over the wall into the garden next door. His neighbours, Terry and Pauline, didn't really take much pride in their garden, so they were not likely to notice, but the main thing, he reasoned, was that even if the snail survived the landing, it was unlikely to find its way back. He picked up the second snail, and that followed its friend over the garden wall. The third one was chucked over a different wall into the garden on the other side for a bit of variety. It was as if Gavin thought that by separating them, they were less likely to conspire together against his plants, but really his thought process was not quite as rational as that; he just wanted rid of them. Satisfied he had seen off the slimy threat for now, he took what was left of his tea back inside and spent the rest of the evening looking up snail prevention methods on his phone.

He found all sorts of suggestions, from pellets to copper tape, all of which looked quite effective but would look quite unsightly and in any case only deterred the little invertebrate swine. He wanted a more permanent, terminal solution. He was amused by the idea of beer traps, a jam jar filled with beer and buried up to its rim, which would attract the snails and they would fall in and drown. The idea of drunken snails being unable to climb out of a jam jar appealed to his sense of humour, but the emptying out of jars filled with beer-sodden snail corpses did not. The simplest solution seemed to be the good, old-fashioned method of pouring salt onto them and watching them shrivel up. The only trouble was that when he went to the kitchen to get some salt out of the cupboard, he was reminded that in an effort to improve their diet, Anthea had started to buy sea salt crystals, which came in their own handy grinder. He tried to imagine himself delicately grinding salt onto the snails and found the whole idea too ridiculous for words. He put the salt grinder back in the cupboard and went back out to the garden to try and come up with a better plan. He would have found it easier to think if Terry and Pauline's grandchildren weren't screaming and yelling in the garden next door. He could only tolerate the noise for a short while before he had to go back inside: he went straight upstairs to the back bedroom so he could look out of the window and see what on earth all the noise was about. He was lucky that his neighbours didn't look after their grandchildren all that often because whenever they did, the tranquillity of the garden was shattered. Gavin didn't mind the children playing outside, but honestly, couldn't they do it quietly?

Today, because it was sunny and warm, the children were delighting in squirting each other with water pistols. They were not, however, the small water pistols Gavin remembered, but huge brightly coloured water guns, more like bazookas than pistols, which sprayed water liberally everywhere. Seeing the children dousing each other suddenly gave him an idea, and he hurried back downstairs. He called to Anthea to let her know he was going out, which elicited a vague acknowledgement he barely heard over the noise of the television, and left the house. He jumped into their old, battered Nissan Micra and drove to the nearest supermarket.

It had been many years since Gavin had shopped for toys, and he was bewildered by the array with which he was presented. Many of the toys on display were based on television shows he had never heard of, and the prices of some of the items were horrifying. He was very glad he no longer had children to buy for; he thought it would probably bankrupt him. All the same, it didn't take him long to find what he was looking for because there was an extensive, shelf-long selection of gaudy, elaborate water guns. They were obviously very popular at this time of year, and the only question was which one to buy. He was drawn to one made of bright green and yellow plastic, which was called Sergeant Saunders' Supershooter (probably another reference to a television show he had never come across). Grabbing the largest packet of salt he could find on the way, he went to the checkout and did his best to ignore the excessive price being demanded for what, when all was said and done, was just a water pistol. He had been ready to say the gun was for his grandson, but the morose youth at the checkout barely registered that he was there at all. He got back into the car, his new acquisitions on the passenger seat beside him, and drove home.

Back in the house, he tore the gun away from its packaging and followed the instructions to fill it. Having satisfied himself that it worked by firing it into the sink until it was empty again, he got down to the business in hand. He took a Pyrex measuring jug out of the cupboard and emptied half of the packet of salt into it, topped it up with water and stirred until, little by little, all the salt crystals had dissolved, leaving a cloudy, white solution. He carefully poured the liquid into the gun and left it by the back door.

By the time the evening came round, the scattering of grey clouds that had been gathering all day had delivered the rain the Met Office had threatened, and the garden was nicely damp— the perfect conditions for Gavin's nocturnal visitors to make what he intended to be their final appearance. He picked up his gun, gave it a shake in case any of the salt had settled, and went outside.

The rain had done its job and the vegetable bed was already full of snails, making their inexorable journeys towards the greenery. Gavin raised his gun, took aim and soaked them with a liberal shower of his saline solution. The effect was instantaneous. As soon as the solution hit the snails, they began to shrivel up. Any that resisted the first dousing were hit by the second. Gavin carried on gleefully firing the gun, feeling like the hero in the action films Anthea never let him watch, until every snail on the vegetable bed was dead. He blew imaginary smoke from the barrel of the gun and, grinning, went back inside. If any more snails arrived to ascertain what had become of their comrades, the ground would be soaked in salt water and hopefully deter them. He would dispose of the empty snail shells in the morning.

He repeated this execution for the next three nights. By the fourth, the snails stopped coming.

The fifth day was miserable and drizzly, and Gavin spent the morning in the shed potting up seedlings, content in the knowledge that they could soon be planted out without fear of molestation. In the afternoon, after a pleasant lunch, he returned to the shed, sat back in his chair, listened to the Test Match for a while and then dozed off. He was fast asleep when the first snail appeared on the shed window, creeping determinedly up the glass, its trail of slime mapping its progress. It was joined by a second, then two more. By the time Gavin had been asleep for half an hour, the window was entirely covered with the sticky snail bodies that adhered to the glass. The inside of the shed was now as dark as evening. Any light which might have seeped in through gaps in the wooden boards and around the door was extinguished by the snails that clung to the outside of the shed, covering every inch of it, preventing not just light getting in, but air too. Gavin slept on, blissfully unaware that the only snails not coating the outside of his shed were the ones that were already inside, oozing across the floor, up the sides of his chair, making their slow and steady progress towards his open mouth.

Anthea didn't hear the muffled screams emanating from the shed or hear when they abruptly stopped. A contestant on one of her favourite game shows was about to go for the jackpot, and she had the volume turned up so she wouldn't miss a second.

"Found in the UK," the host was saying, "what has species called Tawny Glass, White-lipped and Banded?"

Anthea leaned forward in her chair and grinned. She knew the answer to that one.

HANDS

MARTIN RENTON FLEXED the hands that had written three best-selling novels and an acclaimed short story collection and sat with his pen poised over the pad. Then, as he always did, he reached out for his packet of cigarettes and, still looking at the pad, fumbled his way into the packet. There was one cigarette inside. He might write one page on one cigarette, but certainly no more than that. He put the pen down, grabbed his wallet and keys and left the house.

Ordinarily, this would not be the time Martin would choose to go out. There always seemed to be gangs of kids hanging around the off-licence these days. If they didn't ask you to buy booze or cigs for them, they always looked threatening, going quiet as you approached as if daring you to say something. Martin was not a small man, or old or unfit, but still didn't fancy his chances against half a dozen bored teenagers. He always kept his head down as he passed them, making himself invisible and less of a target.

This evening was a warm, pleasant one, and the warmth had multiplied the teenagers. There was a group of at least a dozen outside the off-licence and two smaller groups, one outside the chip shop and one hanging around the bus stop. Realising there was no path which would avoid all of them, Martin found something compelling on the pavement to stare at and walked quickly, but not too quickly, straight into the off-licence. He took his time buying his cigarettes, keeping a vague hope that the gang outside might find somewhere else to be while he was in there.

What happened next was virtually inevitable from the moment Martin left the off-licence and one of the kids asked him for a ciggie. Martin tried to pretend at first that he hadn't heard and walked on, but the kid jogged after him and said again, "Got a ciggie, mate?" Martin was about to claim he didn't have any until the kid added, "I know you just bought some."

"They're not for me." Head still down, Martin kept walking. He only knew that more than one of the gang had followed him when hands grabbed each of his arms.

"Give us a fuckin' ciggie," the first lad said, breathing cider fumes into Martin's face.

"Just take them." Martin hated the whine in his voice. "Have them all."

Days later, lying in hospital, Martin tried to replay in his mind what happened next, but everything from that moment up to the moment he woke up in the hospital bed was blank. Most of what had happened to him he found out from the doctors, but even then, for the first few days he was too groggy to fully understand what they were saying. He had taken a blow to the head, possibly with a brick, and that was why his memory of the event was so vague. It was likely he'd lost consciousness straight away, which was why he had no recollection of the kicking he'd endured that left him with three broken ribs and bruises all over. He certainly couldn't remember them doing what they'd done to his hands. Mr. Snape, the consultant, told him that someone had stood on both hands and literally ground them underfoot. Virtually every bone had been pulverised, tendons snapped like cotton and nerve endings destroyed. In short, Mr. Snape said, it was as if someone had wanted to make damn sure that Martin would never be able to use his hands again. And they had succeeded.

This was the news Martin found hardest to take in. Once he had woken up enough to feel, he could tell his hands were immobilised and that he'd been filled with enough painkillers to make everything numb, but he simply could not comprehend that there was any other reason why his hands wouldn't move. Each time Mr. Snape came to see him, Martin asked when he would be able to use them again, explaining patiently that he was a writer, he *used* his hands, that is what he *did*, and each time, the doctor explained, equally patiently, that the damage was too severe and even micro-surgery would not help. His hands were irredeemably ruined.

Martin refused to believe it. He demanded a second opinion, better drugs, offered to go private, asked to see a physiotherapist, but was told the same thing every time. There was a slim chance he could gain some function by amputation and prosthesis, but it would only be very limited and there was a greater chance that, with the nerve damage, it would not be successful. There was no hope, nothing to be done. He would have to learn how to get by without the use of his hands.

That was probably why he was so prepared to believe Mr. Saunders when he promised a cure.

Martin had no idea who the man was. He had never met him before, never seen him before. His first assumption, when the nurse told him he had a visitor, was that it was another visit from the police. The police had been to see him twice since the attack, once two uniformed officers, once two in plain clothes, but they seemed to have lost interest when they realised how little Martin remembered. When the visitor made his way into the ward and Martin saw his immaculate suit and perfect shoes, he assumed he was a consultant. The man was in his thirties, or perhaps in his forties and took good care of himself. He had tidy, short hair and excellent teeth, which he showed as he smiled broadly and introduced himself as Mr. Saunders. Martin tried to smile back and said, "I'm afraid I can't shake your hand."

"I realise that, and I understand. In fact, that's what I've come to talk to you about. They've said it's permanent, haven't they?"

"Why?" Martin asked, eagerness in his voice as he sensed hope. "Isn't it?"

"Maybe not, but that depends on you."

"I'm sorry, I'm not sure what you mean. Are you a doctor?"

"Nothing needs to be permanent," Saunders said, evading the question. "Tell me, do you believe that there is a connection between your mind and your body? Do you believe that you can, to put it simply, think yourself to better health?"

"Oh, I see," Martin said with a resigned sigh. "You're one of those holistic types. Look, Mr. Saunders, the doctors have told me I'll never be able to use my hands again. I don't think a bit of massage or a few herbs are going to help. So if you don't mind—"

"No, you misunderstand. May I sit down?"

Before Martin could reply, Saunders had made himself comfortable on the chair at the side of the bed. "First of all, let me say that I am not trying to sell anything. I'm merely here to offer my assistance. You see, I *know* there is a strong and powerful connection between the mind and the body, and I'm convinced that you would benefit from it. All I ask is that you trust me."

"Trust you? I don't even know who you are."

"Isn't that where trust comes in?"

"Okay, Mr. Saunders, whoever you are. I'm going to ask you a straight question and I want a straight answer. Can you cure my hands?"

"Straight answer? Yes. I can."

"You wouldn't bullshit me, would you? This is too important to me. If you can't do it and this is some sort of scam, get out now. I'm not messing with this."

"Mr. Renton—sorry, may I call you Martin?" Martin nodded. "Martin, believe me, I am completely serious. I wouldn't mess with something so vital. You have stories and books to be written. Now, you can't do that without your hands, can you? You're much too old school to be dictating. Of course, there is voice

112

recognition software these days, but you can't write any other way than longhand, can you? The words just don't come."

"Old school. Yes, that just about sums me up."

"You need your hands, Martin, and I can give them back to you."

"Then I'll trust you. What do you need me to do?"

"First, I need you to believe me. That's all. There will be something else later, but for now, I just need you to believe me and give me your hands."

"I believe you," Martin said, and in that moment, he meant it with all his heart. He held out his bandage-swathed hands. Saunders reached out and took one hand in each of his.

"You need to start feeling your hands, Martin. Remember how it feels to move your fingers. Remember how it feels to touch things, to hold your pen. If you feel it in your head, you will feel it in your hands. It won't be easy, but it's the only way." He let go of Martin's hands, although Martin hadn't felt it happen and remained with his arms outstretched like a mummy in an old movie.

"Is that it?" he asked.

"That's it as far as I am concerned. It's up to you now. Remember and feel. Do it all the time, with every waking hour. Think of nothing else. I will leave you to concentrate on it now, but I'll be back and you can thank me then."

Without another word, Saunders stood up and left. Martin watched him go and thought, *That's all I need. A bloody crank.* Then he lay back against the pillows and tried to get some sleep. He was suddenly very tired.

He dreamed he had his hands back. In his dream, he was smoking a cigarette, holding it in his hand, raising it to his lips, taking a drag and lowering it again. It was such a simple action, one he had completed many thousands of times, and when he woke, tears were streaming down his face at the lack of it, at the thought that he would only ever do it again in dreams. But when he looked down, his right hand was curled into the inverted C shape it always had when it was holding a cigarette, and between his first two fingers, he fleetingly felt a light, phantom pressure of something there. Then it was gone, and he wanted it back so badly that he thought about what Saunders had said and began to believe.

At first, nothing happened. He concentrated as hard as he could, trying desperately to shut out the hospital noises that surrounded him. He tried to focus his mind on nothing but his hands, striving to remember how it felt to be able to move his fingers, how the muscles felt as they stretched and tensed, how the joints felt as they flexed, but he couldn't do it. Something as natural and habitual as that and he couldn't remember what it felt like. He should have paid more attention when the feeling was there. He dropped his arms back impotently onto the bed, only feeling the soft impact from his wrists up. *It won't be easy*, Saunders had said. He wasn't kidding there.

But Martin refused to give up. Between visits from nurses who wanted to check his blood pressure, temperature, bowel movements and anything else they could come up with to check, he closed his eyes and concentrated. Trying to remember how it felt to move hadn't worked, so he tried the other things Saunders had suggested, to visualise and recall how it felt to touch. He chose the object with which he was most familiar and yet took so much for granted, his Waterman fountain pen, a pen he had owned for over twenty years and which had never let him down. He had spotted it in the window of an antique shop and had been attracted by the silver barrel and cap with its delicate, engine-turned chevron pattern and gold clip, and he'd gone straight into the shop to ask to try it. As soon as he picked it up and felt the weight and the balance of it, he had fallen in love and agreed to buy it without even asking the price.

Now he lay in his hospital bed and tried to recall how it felt between his thumb and his forefinger, how it felt when he wrote, the light resistance of the nib against the paper. He imagined himself signing his name with the flourish he used at the occasional book-signing event. He repeated the image over and over again in his mind, picturing the pen, picturing his hand holding it and then…it was *there*. He felt something against his thigh and when he looked down, his hand was moving, leaving a faint indentation on the bedding, the thumb and finger slightly apart. He was so surprised that he lost concentration and it stopped, but it had definitely, unmistakably been there. His hand had remembered his beloved pen and the impulse to write and moved.

Nobody in the medical profession could quite explain how Martin regained the use of his hands. His consultant, surgeon and his physiotherapist were all at a loss but more than happy to take the credit for it. Martin knew, however, that there was only one person to thank, and the day he was discharged, just over a month since he'd been told he would never use his hands again, he was pleased but not surprised to find Mr. Saunders waiting for him in the hospital foyer.

"This time I can shake your hand," Martin said and did so.

"How are they?" Saunders asked.

"A bit stiff still, but getting there. I don't know how to thank you."

"You did all the hard work, Martin. I just pointed you in the right direction."

"Well, either way, I can never repay you. I can't tell you how grateful I am."

"Funny you should mention that. I don't know if you remember, but I did say that there would be something you could do."

"Anything. Just name it."

Saunders reached into his jacket pocket, took out an envelope and passed it to Martin. Martin opened it and found inside a photograph and a piece of paper with an address written on it. The photograph was of an elderly man coming out of the door of a building and looked like someone watching from across the street had taken it.

"I don't understand," Martin said. "Who's this?"

"You don't need to know his name," Saunders said. "In fact, it's probably better if you don't. All you need to know is that he is a very bad man. He has done some truly evil things in his life, some of them…" and here Saunders glanced around and lowered his voice conspiratorially "…involving children. He is the sort of person the world would be better without. I want you to make sure that is the case. You have his address."

"Wait a minute!" Martin gasped. "Are you asking me to *kill* him?"

"Keep your voice down!" Saunders hissed. "We don't want the nice ladies in the shop to hear."

"No. I'm sorry," Martin said firmly. "I'm not doing that. Are you insane?"

"'Anything,' you said. 'Just name it.'"

"Well, yes, but not *that*! I'm not a murderer."

"And I thought you were grateful. Apparently, I was wrong."

As Saunders said it, Martin felt a searing bolt of pain run through both hands, and they clenched automatically into fists.

"Do you still want to keep your hands?" Saunders asked.

"All right! All right! I'll do it!"

Saunders smiled, and as suddenly as it had arrived, the pain disappeared.

"Excellent. There's no hurry. Any time within the next week should do it."

"A week? I'll need longer than that!"

"To do what? Look for a way to back out? I wouldn't advise that. We have an agreement, and the sooner you keep your side of it, the sooner you can enjoy using your hands again. You have the address there and the key codes, so the doors will not present a problem. He is always in bed just after ten and sleeps heavily, but I would suggest waiting a few hours after that to be sure. How you do it is entirely up to you. You should have a reasonably good imagination, although having read some of your stories, I'm not so sure. A week. I'll be watching."

With that, Saunders turned on his heel and disappeared through the sliding door at the entrance. Martin watched him go, then picked up his belongings and phoned for a taxi to take him home.

He spent the first two days of the week he had been allotted trying to settle back into a house that felt strangely alien to him after so long in hospital. He opened windows to air it and to let out the smell of a loaf that had gone mouldy in the bread bin and milk that had turned rank in the fridge. He cleaned the kitchen and the living room thoroughly, marvelling as he did so at how good it felt to accomplish the most common tasks like dusting and hoovering, things he had once feared he would never do again. But every time he felt good about using his hands, there was a nagging voice at the back of his mind reminding him that it could all be taken away from him again.

The third day, he spent in an unsettling state of inertia. He vacillated between a determination to do Saunders' bidding and then get on with his life, and a terror of the consequences if he should be caught. His hands would do him no good in prison. Caught between the two feelings, he did nothing. On the fourth day, he woke up with a resolve. He would do it, and do it that night. He passed the day getting himself ready, buying disposable latex gloves and batteries for the torch he always kept in the kitchen cupboard but rarely used. As darkness fell, he dressed from head to foot in black, tucked the gloves and torch into his pockets, checked the address and entry codes once more to make sure he had memorised them correctly, then sat waiting until it was late enough to leave the house.

Martin knew the address well. A decade or so earlier, a forward-thinking property developer had purchased several old Victorian warehouses that lined the banks of the canal and had turned them into highly desirable apartments. Each apartment had its own small balcony, and Martin had often envied the view they would afford while realising he would have to sell considerably more books than he was selling before he could even dream of buying one of the apartments. They rarely came on the market, but when they did, they commanded the price of most reasonably sized houses in the area.

Walking the short distance from his house to the apartment complex, Martin was acutely aware of every person he passed and kept his head down, not making eye contact. The complex was mostly in darkness when he got there, just one or two lights behind closed blinds. As he walked hesitantly up the drive, he was startled when a security light flicked on, bathing the drive in dazzling white. He froze, caught between going on and going back, but he had come so far; the only thing he could do was front it out, go straight for the main door and hope there were no CCTV cameras observing his approach. He found the keypad by the side of the door and punched in the numbers he had memorised. There was a click from the lock, and the door opened without a problem.

Inside was a wide communal hall with several large, possibly artificial potted plants and a bank of locked letterboxes, each with an apartment number on it. He paused at the bottom of the stairs and listened. There was the soft whisper of a television coming from one apartment, and quiet music coming from somewhere else, but otherwise no sign of life. The apartment he was looking for was at the top of the building, so he began to climb the stairs. He was halfway up before he realised he was holding his breath.

At the top of the stairs was a landing with another of the potted plants (he wondered briefly if the owners of the building had got a job lot somewhere) and a window that looked out onto the canal below. There was a door at either end of the landing, and his torch picked out the number 18—the apartment he was looking for—on the one on the left. He was relieved to see no light leaking out under the door; it looked very much as though Saunders was right and the apartment's occupant had indeed retired for the night. Trying not to think about the reason he was there, Martin entered the code on the pad by the apartment door, and as slowly and quietly as he could, he opened the door.

There was enough light from outside bleeding in through the drawn blinds for him to be able to see well enough without his torch, which was a blessing. The apartment, as far as he could see, was every bit as luxurious as he had expected. The door opened onto a large living area which had been comfortably and tastefully furnished. At one end was an immaculate kitchen area with a dining table situated next to a set of blind-free sliding doors that looked out onto the balcony with its panoramic view over the canal. There were several doors off the living area, which presumably led to the bedrooms and possibly a bathroom, but they were all shut so it was not possible to tell which was which.

Martin paused in the middle of the living room and looked around, trying to get the measure of the man he was here to kill. He didn't know what the 'terrible things' Saunders had mentioned were and in truth had given little thought to it, but this was an apartment that showed affluence and good taste. Perhaps its owner was a criminal and this place had been furnished with the profits of other people's misery, but if that were the case, it had been surprisingly easy to get in. One would have thought such a person would have had tighter security. Martin wondered for a second if maybe the apartment was being watched, but if it was, any guards who were lurking around would surely have been up here by now. The thought of it made him listen intently for any sound of footsteps on the stairs, but there was nothing. The apartment was silent, and the silence made him uneasy. Now he understood that old film cliché about it being 'too quiet', and it was this feeling of unease that prompted him to get on with it and find the man he was supposed to kill.

The first door he tried led into what was presumably the guest bedroom. It had two stripped single beds, two bedside cabinets and a dressing table. Wardrobes were built into the walls, but the room was obviously not currently being used. Martin closed the door, making as little noise as he could, and tried the next one. This was clearly the main bedroom, as it was dominated by a king-size, or possibly even super-king-size bed. There were clothes on the back of a chair, and one of the built-in wardrobes was partially open. The room itself, however, was unoccupied, and it dawned on Martin why the apartment was so quiet: there was nobody in residence at all. If the apartment's owner was out for the night, then they could return at any time. That made the situation so risky, his best option would be to get out and either return at a later date or rethink the whole idea.

Martin left the master bedroom and headed for the entrance door. As he did so, he heard the last sound he wanted to hear; someone was punching the code into the keypad outside the door. In a panic, Martin looked around for somewhere to hide. There was only one place he could think of. He hurried to the sliding doors that led out onto the balcony, fully expecting them to be locked and considerably relieved to find that they weren't. He slipped out onto the balcony and slid the door shut behind him. Then he waited.

Doing his best to flatten himself against the outside wall while staying in a position from which he could see inside, he watched the wedge of light widen as the front door opened and the silhouette of a figure entered the apartment. Nothing could have prepared him for what he saw when the figure emerged into the half-light. It wasn't the man he had seen in the photograph, the owner of the apartment, the person he had almost casually been prepared to kill. It was the man he had spoken to at the hospital and who had given him hope, the one who called himself Saunders. Martin wanted to go straight into the apartment and have a furious confrontation with him, but the rational half of his brain told him that was probably not a good idea and it was best to keep hidden. Saunders, however, had other plans and took the choice out of his hands by crossing the kitchen area and sliding the door open.

"Aren't you a bit chilly out there, Martin?"

"What the hell are you doing here? He's out. That man, whoever he is, he's out. He could come back any minute."

"No, he won't," Saunders said. "The owner of this apartment moved in with his girlfriend a few weeks ago. He hasn't got around to putting it on the market yet. I suspect he's having second thoughts and needs somewhere to come back to when it all goes wrong. He certainly won't be coming back tonight."

"Then what am I doing here? What's going on, Saunders?"

"That is the question, isn't it? I really think it would be better if you came inside. It may rain."

"I'm fine here. Now tell me what the *fuck* is going on."

"Fine. Have it your way. I must admit that I haven't exactly told you the truth."

"Really?"

"Don't be sarcastic. A writer like you should know it is the lowest form of wit. The man who owns this lovely apartment is an architect. He hasn't, as I suggested, ever done anything terrible, unless you call an over-reliance on recreational drugs and the occasional one-night stand terrible things. Personally, I say each to his own. Whatever gets you through the day."

"Then why did you want me to kill him?"

"Martin, it's going to be a very long night if you don't at least make the effort to keep up. I didn't want you to kill him. If I wanted him dead, why would I send you at a time when I knew he wouldn't be here? That doesn't make sense."

"Then why am I here?"

"I suppose you could call it an experiment. A test. I wanted to establish what you would be prepared to do to keep your hands, and I must admit, I'm quite surprised. I didn't expect you to go through with it. Clearly, I underestimated the size of a writer's ego. I didn't think that was possible."

"What is it you want, Saunders?"

"Martin, I really wouldn't try to sound threatening when you're the one skulking around outside. I wanted to see if you were the right person for a job I have in mind. I had to see how far you'd go, and it looks like I picked the right person."

"I'm not doing anything else for you. You lied to me about this. How do I know—"

"It's a writing job."

"A *writing* job? What sort of a writing job? Because I don't do commercial work."

"I thought that would get your interest. I have a book I need writing, and for various reasons I can't go into now, I am unable to do it myself. It's a rather special book, and there would be a certain amount of risk involved. That's why I needed this test of how far you would go."

Martin leaned on the balcony rail with both hands, looking out over the canal. In the distance, someone was calling for their dog, but otherwise the night was quiet.

"No, sorry," he said finally. "I've got enough of my own work to do and I'm behind on that. I can't do it."

"Your work?" Saunders laughed. "*Your* work? Your work is garbage, Martin. Your plots are nothing that hasn't been written a hundred times before, and by better people. Your prose is turgid, and your dialogue is frankly embarrassing. I'm not really sure how you got published in the first place."

"I've had three bestsellers…" Martin began indignantly, but Saunders just laughed again.

"I would have thought you were more intelligent than to measure quality by sales. Any lobotomised chimp who has been on the television can have a bestseller. I'm not talking about sales, Martin. I'm talking about a book that could make you immortal."

"No. Sorry. I'm not interested."

"I'm disappointed. I thought you might have the imagination to want something better than you have. So be it."

"That's it? I can go?"

"Go? Did I say that? No, Martin, you can't go. We had a deal. You said you would do anything to keep your hands, remember? And you haven't done anything."

"I came here, didn't I? I did what you asked. I would have done more." As he spoke, Martin backed away to the furthest point of the balcony until the cast iron rail dug into his back. He glanced over his shoulder. The apartment was much too high up to jump; if he didn't land in the canal, the fall would kill him, but maybe there was somewhere he could climb to.

"There's no point looking," Saunders said. "There's nowhere for you to go. Even if there was, there's nowhere you could hide that I wouldn't find you. All I have to decide is whether I'm going to take your hands or your life."

"You stay back! I'll call the police—"

"And say what? You've broken into someone else's home! Do you want me to remind you why you came here?"

Saunders stepped out onto the balcony and advanced. Glancing over his shoulder again, Martin spotted a drainpipe running down between this balcony and the one belonging to the flat next door. There might be someone there who could help. Holding onto the wall, he managed to climb up onto the balcony rail and swayed unsteadily, but the grip he had on the corner of the wall kept him upright. He reached out his left hand and grabbed hold of the drainpipe, praying it would take his weight, then swung his body around and reached for the balcony rail next door with his foot. At first, his foot only found thin air, but he kicked out again and felt the rail under his instep. He clung to the wall and the drainpipe, his face pressed into the brickwork, and heard Saunders' voice coming from somewhere nearby.

"It's at times like this that you really need your hands," Saunders said.

It started as a sharp pain in the back of both hands, as if a knife had been plunged in deep between the bones of his fingers. Then he heard a crunch and screamed as the bones separated and, one by one, the tendons and nerves snapped like over-tightened guitar strings. The last thing he felt was a cold numbness creeping up his hands and barely had time to register the fact that at least it was taking the pain away before he let go and fell. He landed on his back, and his head hit the concrete edge of the canal bank. Dazed, he tried to get to his feet, but his hands were useless, and he stumbled backwards and fell into the icy, black water of the canal. He flailed hopelessly but couldn't grab anything to keep him up and he sank.

Within two weeks of Martin Renton's death—by suicide, it was assumed, due to the tragic loss of the use of his hands—all three of his books were rapidly reassessed as classics of their genre and flew back up to the top of the bestseller charts, where they remained for several weeks until a celebrity chef brought out a new diet book and they dropped back down the charts as rapidly as they had risen. They appeared in the discount bins of some bookshops and as a buy-one-get-one-free offer in a chain of book-clearance shops for a while and then, like their author, disappeared altogether.

SCHOOL
PHOTOGRAPH

T HE DAY AFTER Dixie's funeral, Ian Doyle noticed there were people missing from his old school photograph, and Dixie was just one of them.

Ian had not given the photograph the slightest thought for many years. It had languished rolled up in the bottom of a wardrobe in a box he had rescued from his parents' house after his father died. He had spent one drunken night after Anna had gone to bed looking through the old family photos, filled with post-funeral nostalgia. The next day, while Ian slept off his hangover, Anna had put the box away in the wardrobe and it had stayed there ever since. It was only when Dixie died that Ian remembered the school photo was there at all. Even Anna had forgotten it was in the wardrobe in the spare room, and normally, she remembered where everything was.

The photograph was one of those long, whole-school photos with the teachers all sitting at the front, the headmaster in the middle. The pupils were all tiered behind, oldest at the front, youngest at the back. It was the sort of photograph private schools took every so often and hung in frames along the corridors.

Ian could vaguely remember the day it was taken. It was a sunny day, and the school all trooped out onto the playing field, where an elaborate construction of scaffold and benches had been built. The boys were all arranged in their years and told to keep still while the photographer swung his camera along the rows for the panoramic shot. It was rumoured that a boy on one end of a row could jump down and run along the back before the camera reached the other end and so appear on the picture twice, but as far as Ian knew, no one had ever tried it.

The photographer, a man in his fifties, had no idea how to deal with a school full of boys who didn't really want to be there and was very much lacking in patience. More than once he had snapped at pupils who weren't in quite the right place and on one occasion shouted at Mr. Snowdon, the young chemistry teacher. Mr. Snowdon had only joined the school that year, and everybody shouted at him. The picture taken, everyone trooped back into their classrooms and the teachers took orders for overpriced prints. Ian remembered the day the prints were delivered. He took his home and with his parents scanned the faces for his own. Then the photograph was rolled up, put away and forgotten about.

Dixie—Graham Dixon—had been the class clown. His jokes were always good-natured, always just within the rules while making the other boys (and often the teachers) laugh. Ian, much quieter and more studious, looked up to him. They had become friends when Dixie spotted Ian reading a dog-eared copy of *The Hitchhiker's Guide to the Galaxy* in a break, and in the ensuing conversation, they had discovered a shared love of Monty Python, the Goons and Doctor Who. They had remained firm friends throughout their time at school, gradually losing touch when they had gone to different universities.

Years later, when Anna had introduced Ian to Facebook, Ian had found Dixie, now living in Dover and headteacher of a primary school, of all things. In his profile picture, he was still recognisable as Dixie, though his once-unruly spiky fair hair was now grey, much like Ian's own. They had exchanged messages and shared posts and even made vague plans to meet up again one day. Then a post appeared on Dixie's timeline that made Ian feel like the floor had fallen away beneath him. Dixie's family had posted a message to all his Facebook friends announcing that regrettably Graham Dixon had passed away suddenly from a heart attack. Ian took the day off work and travelled to Dover for the funeral. He knew nobody there and slipped away straight after the service. By the time he got home late that night, he was tired and sad. Dixie was the first of his contemporaries to die.

Being the only person from the old days to attend Dixie's funeral was probably what prompted Ian to look for the school photograph. While Anna was out, he unrolled it on the living room table and studied the faces. It was just as he remembered, even down to the name of the photographer, Saunders, at the bottom. He found his fourteen-year-old self towards the middle, wearing a very artificial smile. His tie was slightly crooked—he remembered his mother's reaction to that.

"Only one photograph, and you couldn't even keep your tie straight."

Next to Ian was Steve Bradley, with whom Ian exchanged a nod and an 'all right' when they passed in the corridor but who hung out with the computer guys in the maths room at breaks. Next to Steve was Nick McBain, with his dark hair cut in a style that, should future generations happen upon it, placed the photograph firmly in the early 1980s. McBain hung around with another Nick, whose surname Ian could not recall but might have been Ronson, and The Two Nicks, as they were universally known, were the coolest lads in the year. They were into music that no one else had heard of and wanted to form a band. Ian had no idea if they ever did. He briefly looked on the photo for the other Nick but couldn't spot him. Maybe he was off that day.

It was when Ian tried to find Dixie on the photo that he started to feel like his memory was playing tricks. Dixie, he was sure, had been on the row behind him. Yes, he was certain of that because just as the picture was being taken, Dixie had muttered that he was within kicking range of Ian's arse. In the photo, Ian could see himself turning to reply, but when he looked along the row of faces behind his, there was John Brookes, Gordon Dent (known as 'Arthur' to Ian and Dixie), another lad whose name Ian couldn't remember, Joe Miller...but no Dixie. Ian rubbed his tired eyes. He was about to have another look when Anna came home from her Zumba class. He rolled the photograph back up and put it in a corner, resolving to look at it again when he had more time.

The photograph would probably have stayed in the corner until Anna got fed up with it and tidied it away again, had drugs not claimed the life of Vic Liddell. Ian was half-watching the news one night when, amid reports of the latest unrest in the Middle East, he saw that Liddell had been found dead. Liddell had been the lead singer of The Promised Land, pioneers of the eighties synth-pop movement. The band had not been to Ian's taste, he preferred the sound of guitars to synthesisers, but he was more than aware of their songs. He had not known, however, that Liddell had been brought up in the same part of Liverpool as Ian and went to the nearby comprehensive school.

The report flashed back through Liddell's career and showed a picture of Liddell's first band, Undercurrent, which he had formed while still at school. There, standing next to Liddell, fringe in his eyes, was the one of The Two Nicks who wasn't Nick McBain. Ian called the internet up on his phone and googled Undercurrent. The band had formed in 1982 and, despite splitting up in 1984 without having a hit, still seemed to have a fan following, probably due to Vic Liddell having gone on to much greater things. But it was the reason the band had split up that made Ian pull the school photograph out again. Undercurrent had, it seemed, fallen apart shortly after the untimely death of guitarist Nick Robson (*Robson, that was it!*) when his motorcycle came off second best against a lorry on the M62. The band had, with the exception of Vic Liddell, promptly been consigned to the history books, along with all the other bands who should have been great but weren't.

So Ian unrolled the photograph again and looked for Nick Robson. Thinking back, he was sure Robson had been there. He and McBain were inseparable in those days, and he could even vaguely remember having seen them standing next to each other in the picture, two haircuts daring for their day amid a sea of normal side or front partings. But when Ian found Nick McBain again, he had 'Arthur' Dent on one side of him and another lad whose name Ian couldn't remember on the other. Nick Robson was nowhere to be seen. Yet Ian's mind's eye pictured The Two Nicks sauntering across the playing field, hands in their pockets as usual, on their way to line up for the photograph. Maybe he was wrong. Maybe he was just picturing them like that because that was how they always walked around the school. It was over thirty years ago, after all.

Ian lay awake in bed that night wondering about it. First Dixie, now Robson. Both dead and neither of them even remembered on their old school photograph. As Ian was drifting off to sleep, a sudden thought hit him that rendered him wide awake. He didn't remember seeing Jason Kelly on the photograph either, and he was definitely there.

Ian had not given Jason Kelly the slightest thought for many years, despite how famous Kelly had been at the time and for all the wrong reasons. He was a council estate boy at a fee-paying school. His parents had sacrificed everything to raise the money for the fees and so could only afford to send him to school in second-hand uniforms. This made him stand out amongst his already fashion-conscious peers and led to name-calling and bullying. He led a solitary existence, with no one wanting to become victim to the same sneering by befriending him. Ian, to his shame, also shunned Kelly and joined in with the mickey-taking. But this was not why Jason Kelly became famous. His fame came from being one of the very rare pupils to be expelled for sniffing glue in the school toilets. Not only was he expelled, but he was also made an example of in an assembly that was called by the headmaster on a Friday afternoon. The rest of the boys were left with no doubt that anyone caught abusing solvents would face a similar fate. Worse was to come for Jason Kelly. He was found several weeks later by his father, dead in his bedroom, a plastic bag of Evo-stick stuck to his face. He was the talk of the school for a while after, but then something or other became the hot topic and Kelly was forgotten.

Jason Kelly was there when the school photograph was taken; Ian was certain because nobody wanted to be photographed standing next to him. There were such protests raised and so much disruption caused by poor Jason Kelly being pushed from one place to another that Mr. Ratcliffe, the deputy head, had to get involved. He compromised by placing Kelly on the end of a row so that only one person (a fourth year called Williams who was given no choice) had to stand next to him.

Unable to sleep, Ian crept downstairs and looked at the photograph again. There was Williams, on the end of a row, looking distinctly uncomfortable. Of Jason Kelly, there was no sign.

Ian, usually a heavy sleeper, slept badly that night. The next morning, he got up earlier than usual to give himself plenty of time before he had to go to work. Locating the magnifying glass he kept in a drawer in the kitchen (because sometimes the instructions on things were clearly designed for younger eyes than his), he took it upstairs to the spare room and unrolled the school photograph. Everything was as he remembered it the night before. He was relieved to see that all the same faces were in the same places, as far as he could recall. There was nobody missing. But as he went to roll up the photograph again, he noticed there was something wrong with Steve Bradley.

Bradley was still in the photograph, next to Ian. Just looking at him reminded Ian that the lad's personal hygiene had not been all it should be. The rest of the lads in their year were reaching an age where their thoughts were consumed by fashion, hair gel and the range of deodorant sprays that were coming onto the market. Ian remembered how grown up he'd felt when his father presented him with his first deodorant and talcum powder set. It was a make called Blue Stratos, and he could still smell it now, even though the make itself had long gone.

At the time of the school photo, the obsession with pubescent grooming hadn't quite made it to Steve Bradley, and it was generally felt that it was not a good idea to sit anywhere near him after sports lessons. Even though they were all supposed to take a shower after sports, Bradley either skipped the shower altogether or was waterproof because it didn't seem to make much difference. From the distance of years, Ian felt the same relief he had back then, when the momentous school photo fell after a maths lesson rather than PE.

And there Steve Bradley was, but he didn't look right. It took Ian a moment or two to work out exactly what was wrong, but when he realised, it was obvious. Something had gone amiss in either the taking or the development of the photograph because through the upper half of Steve Bradley, he could see the faint outline of the lower half of Graham Dent standing behind him. He wondered briefly if all the copies of the photograph had been like that, or if, typically, he'd got the only faulty one, but he stopped short. That was ridiculous. It was the person standing right next to him. Surely he would have noticed before. His parents would certainly have noticed at the time; they'd complained enough about how much the photograph cost and wouldn't have accepted one that was anything less than perfect. His parents were not mean by any standards, but they were, as his dad always pointed out, careful, and that was different. No, unlikely as it sounded, the image of Steve Bradley had started to fade from the photograph.

Ian opened and closed the Facebook app on his phone three times before taking the plunge and searching for Steve Bradley's profile. It didn't help that it was a fairly common name. There were plenty of Steve Bradleys, as well as numerous Stephens and Stevens (Ian didn't know which variant *his* Steve was short for). The intervention of the years also made it difficult for him to recognise a face he hadn't seen in over thirty years from the miniature profile pictures, and not everybody used a picture of themselves anyway. He narrowed the search by entering the name of the school alongside Bradley's, and it came back with a single result, a profile at which Ian had already glanced but rejected as looking nothing like the Steve Bradley he remembered. He pictured a boy with brown hair that came as close to his shoulders as the school would allow, a boy who struggled and failed to keep his weight down and was sometimes picked on for being fat when in reality he only carried a little more weight than his peers. The man in the profile picture was completely bald and his face was thin to the point of being gaunt.

A quick read of his posts told Ian why. Steve Bradley was in the advanced stages of pancreatic cancer. Chemotherapy and radiotherapy had failed to help, and according to his most recent post, dated only three days previously, his consultant had told him it was a matter of time, and not a great amount of time at that. Ian logged out of Facebook, rolled up the school photograph and put it back in the wardrobe. At some point very soon, Steve Bradley would vanish completely and Ian didn't want to know it had happened.

He didn't tell Anna about the photograph. Unless you wanted to be sent straight to a doctor or a therapist, it wasn't the sort of thing you told people about. On the occasions when Anna asked him why he appeared distracted, he made vague comments about pressures of work, and generally she asked no more than that.

After a while, he thought about it less and less and might never have thought about is again if it hadn't been for the headaches.

They started just after Christmas, the first one in years where Ian and Anna had been able to take more than a week off at the same time. Normally, one of them had to work at least a day or two over the Christmas period, but they'd both finished on Christmas Eve and were not due back in until 2nd January. They were able to socialise, have late nights and lie-ins and consequently overdid it completely, which was why Ian paid little attention to the headaches at first. It was bad for a day and then nagged for a further day, but by the time Ian was back and fully immersed in work, it had gone completely.

Once the world woke up after the holidays and work started to get busy again, Ian began to get headaches every couple of weeks. Sometimes they were only a dull throb behind his right eye, and sometimes they felt like someone was poking his brain with a knife, but he swallowed down a couple of the painkillers he carried around in his pocket and they went away again. It was only when he went to the kitchen one night to get a drink to take another couple of tablets (he had one of the dull headaches and the television was shouting at him), that Anna finally said something.

"Another headache?"

"Just a bit of one. Long day."

"You're getting a lot of them, aren't you?"

Ian paused before gulping the tablets down. Up until that moment, he hadn't really thought about it. The headaches were just *there* and dealt with.

"A few," he said. "It's been busy. I've been staring at a screen a lot."

"Do you think you could do with getting your eyes tested? You might need glasses."

"Oh God, I'm getting old! It'll be false teeth next."

"There's nothing wrong with glasses. Anyway, the opticians can tell all sorts these days. Might be best to get checked out, just in case—"

"There's nothing wrong with me!" Ian snapped. "Sorry. There really isn't."

"If you say so, but I'm worried about you. That packet of paracetamol was full last week. It's nearly empty now."

"Honestly, I'm fine." Ian chose not to mention that he'd only gone in the cupboard because he'd used the last of the tablets he kept in his pocket earlier that day. "I'll get my eyes tested, though. I'll make an appointment tomorrow."

Anna nodded and went back to watching the television. He knew she didn't believe him, but she wouldn't remind him again if he were careful about how many painkillers he took around her. In truth, he had already decided against going anywhere near the opticians, especially if, as Anna had said, they could 'tell all sorts'. There was nothing wrong with him, and he didn't want to be told there was. He had always been of the opinion that doctors and dentists, and now opticians apparently, had to find *something* to justify their existence. After all, if there was nothing wrong with you, there would be no prescription or treatment to pay for, and that wouldn't benefit anyone. He knew people who went to the doctor over the slightest thing, but he had never been one of them and didn't intend to start now.

The headaches continued but didn't get any more frequent (or did they?), and Ian continued to hide them. All the same, Anna's suggestion that there might be something there for an optician to spot worried him. He had seen plenty of stories about people being struck down by bleeds on the brain they'd dismissed as headaches, or who had been diagnosed too late with tumours they'd put down to stomach ache. But he was equally convinced that these people were simply unlucky and that sort of thing would never happen to him. He was healthy for his age, didn't smoke, took moderate exercise and ate the sorts of foods that were always being recommended. There was no reason to think the headaches were anything other than exactly that.

He had the first dream in February. In it, he was transported back to his schooldays, although when Ian Doyle climbed up onto the bench to take his place in the school photograph, it was the fifty-three-year-old Ian he saw in his mind's eye, not the fourteen-year-old version. Steve Bradley was already there on the bench, but it was a haggard man with only a few wispy tufts of hair left who stood there, bizarrely in school uniform. He turned to look at Ian, and his eyes were milky with cataracts. He stank, but not of body odour; it was a stench of decay that no deodorant could counter.

Someone was calling Ian's name, wanting to know where he was, and he tried to open his mouth to say, "I'm here!" but a wave of pain assaulted his head and he couldn't speak. He woke up drenched in perspiration to find Anna calling his name. He told her he'd had a bad dream, went to the bathroom to wash his face and then went back to sleep, this time without dreams. Anna didn't mention the dream at breakfast, but Ian was aware she was regarding him warily, and he couldn't leave for work fast enough. He put the dream out of his head and forgot about it for a week. Then he had another one.

He was on the landing in the darkness and dressed, not in the T-shirt he wore to bed, but in his work clothes of shirt and tie. He knew, in the way one knows things in dreams, that something had woken him up and he had come to investigate. Somewhere, he could hear whispers, not one voice, but several. He couldn't make out what they were saying or where they were coming from, but as he crept across the landing, he identified the source of the sound. It was coming from behind the closed door of the spare bedroom. Cautiously, he opened the door and the whispers grew louder. He still couldn't hear exactly what they were saying, but within the hiss of voices, he heard his name. He stood in the gloom, the glow of the streetlight outside the window permeating the gaps in the blinds and casting odd, geometric shadows.

The whispering was coming from the wardrobe. He didn't want to open it. He had no desire to find out what was causing the sound but was compelled to do so. In the wardrobe, lying where he had left it on top of a couple of old boxes of books, was the school photograph, and the whispers were the voices of classmates he had not heard for years. He picked up the photograph with trembling hands, his heart thumping like a half-heard bass line, but before he could roll it out, the photograph jerked violently, and a skeletal hand half-covered in shreds of rotting skin shot out and seized his wrist. This time, he woke up screaming and Anna had to hold him until his heart slowed to something like its regular rhythm. She was asleep again long before he was.

The following day was a Sunday and Ian was up early. He eased himself out of bed, trying hard not to wake his wife and, after going to the bathroom, stood still on the landing, listening. He could hear the faint sound of early morning traffic outside and the dawn chorus of a particularly vocal blackbird, but there were no phantom whispers or indeed any other sound coming from the spare bedroom. All the same, he had his hand on the door handle before he knew what he was doing but caught himself in time and went downstairs to make a cup of coffee and take some tablets to fend off the headache that was starting to gnaw at the right side of his head.

Several times during that day he talked himself out of going upstairs to look at the photograph. The possibility that his image, like that of Steve Bradley, might be fading from the picture was too much to accept. Each time, he convinced himself that dreams meant nothing and he was being ridiculous. Perhaps it was a mistake to have the several glasses of wine to which he normally treated himself at the weekend.

It might well have been the wine that made him feel bolder, but whatever it was, while Anna sat downstairs watching *The Antiques Roadshow*, he went slowly upstairs into the spare bedroom and took the school photograph out of the wardrobe.

No one ever really knew what happened the next day. The only thing that was certain was that on his way to work, Ian stepped off the platform and into the path of an oncoming train. Shocked witnesses were convinced he had stepped and not fallen, but there was no rational explanation why. His stunned widow told the police they had been perfectly happy, that he had no more pressure at work than other people, that he certainly hadn't shown any suicidal tendencies. She never mentioned the headaches, and the autopsy didn't find any physical cause. The reasons for Ian Doyle's death would remain a mystery, as would why, exactly, he had been carrying an old school photograph rolled up in his coat pocket. The thing Anna found most inexplicable was why Ian had the photograph at all. As she discovered one lonely, tear-stained evening, after an hour of scouring the lines of faces, Ian hadn't even been in school on the day the photograph was taken. Why on earth would you keep a school photograph on which you didn't even appear?

THE CAT CREPT
OUT AGAIN

BILL AND LIZZIE called the cat Boo, and it suited her. That wasn't her full name, but it was the one that fitted and she was rarely called anything else. When they had adopted her from the rescue centre, she was a small, frightened ball of calico fluff, so thin that her ears and eyes were huge and she looked like a cat in an Egyptian statue. She had, they were told, come from the house of one of those Mad Cat Women, who feel it is their mission in life to adopt every cat they can and then, when the cats inevitably breed, find they are overrun and cannot give all the cats the love and care that was the idea in the first place. Bill and Lizzie had fallen in love with this one at first sight and hadn't looked at any others.

They'd never thought about adopting a cat before but had reached a point in their lives, childless but with a great deal of love to give, when it seemed like a good idea. They had visited one animal shelter first, but the staff had not been interested enough to talk to them, and the cats they saw, while undoubtedly beautiful, had not grabbed their hearts. Lizzie had come across Take Me Home by chance. It was a much smaller organisation, and she had warmed to the owner while talking on the phone. The owner of the centre came to their house to see them; after listening to all they had to say, she agreed that an indoor cat would suit them well and told them she would let them know as soon as a suitable cat came in. She rang three days later and said that a cat had arrived that they might want to see. They hurried round straight away. Lizzie went into the pen first and was in there a long time, while Bill made small talk with the owner outside. When Lizzie finally emerged, her eyes were shining.

"Go and see her," she said.

Bill went into the pen and couldn't see a cat at all at first. Then a head emerged from under the cat bed, and Bill looked into the most startling yellow-green eyes he had ever seen. They were the colour of peridots, huge and piercing. He spent a little time talking to the cat and then came out to where his wife was waiting expectantly. He didn't need to say anything. A nod was enough.

They had taken the cat home three days later, and she made pathetic, soft yowling noises all the way. Following the advice they'd been given, they kept the cat in the cage in which she had travelled in the kitchen, furnished her with a bed, food and water and left her on her own as much as they could to settle. When they went to bed that night, there was a cat in the cage. The following morning, when Bill came down first to put the kettle on, the cage was empty. In a panic, he hunted high and low, but it was only when he heard a scuffling under the kitchen unit and pulled the kickboard away that he found the cat, cowering in the furthest corner. He made reassuring noises and tried to coax her out, but if she could have got through the wall to get further away, she would have done. He left the kickboard off the unit and resolved to let the poor thing find her own way out. She would come out for the food when she was hungry, but there was no point now in trying to keep her in the cage. She had got out once, though Bill would never know how, and would doubtless do it again.

Over the next few days, they saw very little of the cat, which they had called Caboodle, after Lizzie had joked that she was 'the whole kitten caboodle', and the name stuck. Because she made such infrequent appearances and at such unexpected times,

Caboodle was rapidly shortened to Boo, and that was pretty much that. They kept the kitchen door closed, understanding that their large house might be a bit bewildering for a small cat, and talked to her when she appeared, but she always shot off under the kitchen unit when any humans came near.

For over a week they only caught fleeting glimpses of her retreating form, but one Sunday, Bill was in the living room while Lizzie was preparing dinner in the kitchen, and he heard his wife say, "Oh, hello!" He crept cautiously into the kitchen to see Lizzie crouched on the floor, smiling through tears, as a small calico cat sniffed tentatively at her outstretched hand. Bill gently picked up a bag of cat treats they kept close by in case of such an occurrence and tossed a couple onto the floor. Boo sniffed them suspiciously then wolfed them down. As soon as she had, she decided that this was enough human contact for one day and darted back under the unit, but Bill and Lizzie were confident it would only be a matter of time.

That was three years ago, and the little frightened cat was unrecognisable. She had put on weight and her ears no longer seemed quite so big. Her eyes were still arresting but were now in proportion with the rest of her head. She wasn't fat, despite Bill's exaggerated *oof!* every time she landed on him, which was often. She was now the most beautiful and devoted animal, and they couldn't imagine life without her. When they were sitting down in the evening, she sat next to or on one of them, slumbering and purring contentedly. If either of them got up, especially Lizzie, she would prick up her ears, then stretch in a dramatic manner and follow. If either of them was under the weather or feeling low, Boo was always there to comfort, sitting close by or cuddling up, gazing at them with those incredible eyes, holding their gaze in a way cats weren't really supposed to do. "She *knows*," they often said, and they meant it. Their cat had an incredible and touching empathy. Lizzie summed it up one day with a phrase that stayed with Bill for a long time after.

"It's like she can see into our souls."

***

The virus changed all that.

2020 started as pretty much every year started, with promises that this would be *their* year, that all the bad stuff from the previous year would be erased and it would be a brand-new beginning. For a few weeks, it even looked like it might be true. Bill welcomed some promising new customers to his computer supplies shop, and Lizzie continued to be happy at the library where she worked. The stories coming out of China of a virus were only background noise. But little by little, that noise grew louder. The papers printed stories that this virus, now given the tame-sounding name of coronavirus, was on its way to Europe, to Britain, and was, as the journalists insisted on describing it, 'potentially deadly'. Just about everyone Bill spoke to dismissed it as a bad cold, nothing much to worry about, a lot of fuss about nothing, scaremongering. There was even talk of conspiracy theories, that an unpopular government was somehow trying to con the public and the whole thing was an experiment to see how far the people could be scared into compliance. Even if it was real, it was only going to be serious in a small number of cases—the elderly, those who already had health issues, people for whom a bad bout of flu would be just as serious. For the general population, it would be somewhere between nothing at all and an unpleasant week or two off work. Bill and Lizzie were quite happy to dismiss it as media hysteria until the first cases in Britain and then the first deaths were announced. Then the figures started to climb and it got very serious indeed.

Bill monitored the news closely, still hoping against hope that it would all blow over before it came to a point where he would have to close the shop. He was very much aware that if the business were not taking money, the rent and bills would still have to be found somewhere, and while there was some money in the bank, it would not last more than a month or two. He watched the news night after night with an increasing feeling of disbelief as the world began, little by little, to close down. In the meantime, Britain appeared to have lost its collective mind. The supermarkets were selling out of tinned goods, pasta, cleaning products and toilet roll quicker than they could restock the shelves. The news reports were full of footage of desperate customers piling trolleys, of fights breaking out for the last pack of toilet roll, of shortages of bottled water. The reports of the greed of his fellow humans exasperated Bill.

"Why toilet roll?" he asked Lizzie one evening. "Nowhere does it say that the screaming shits are a symptom of this thing. And what's the water all about? It's called coronavirus, not cholera, for God's sake. Turn on a bloody tap!"

It was looking very much like lockdown was now inevitable. Lockdown. A phrase, like 'underlying health conditions', that most people had never uttered before and now used all the time. But beneath it all, increasing numbers of people were dying and the inevitable became real. Over the course of one weekend, bookended by government announcements, the country closed down and its citizens were banished to their homes and told to stay there. Bill and Lizzie spent much of that weekend in supermarket queues, forced into panic-buying along with everyone else. On the Monday, ahead of the official instruction to do so, Bill closed the shop. He packed some of the more valuable items into the boot of his car, set the alarm, pulled down the shutters and drove away from the business in which he had invested so much time and effort, with no idea when, or indeed if, he would return. That night, with Lizzie on one side of him holding his hand,

and Boo on the other, staring at him with her sweet peridot eyes, he wept.

Over the next few days, things began to look a little better. Bill and Lizzie slept in, watched television, started to read the books they hadn't got around to, and it felt like the holiday they had not been able to take for so long. Boo loved the extra attention she was getting so much, Lizzie joked that maybe the whole virus thing had been engineered by cats so they could keep their people home a bit more. They were lucky, they told each other over and over again; they had a nice house, they had each other, and above all, they had their health. There were so many people in much worse situations than they were.

After two weeks, boredom began to set in. They had read the books they had never got around to reading and watched the films they recorded at Christmas and never found the time to watch. They had played countless games of rummy and Scrabble, and the novelty of the time off was wearing thin. It felt like the world was on pause, waiting for something to happen, a miracle that would release everyone from captivity and let things get back to whatever kind of normal there was left. On his darkest days, Bill would sometimes remark that he wished he would just get the damn virus so he could get over it and be done. Every day, the count of the dead grew higher until it was just numbers to which they were growing numb. Sometimes they talked sadly about how many people they knew who would simply not be there anymore when this was all over, but most of the time they remained thankful that they, and all those they loved, were still alive and safe. They would, they said, rather be bored than the alternative.

It might have carried on that way had Boo not somehow contrived to upend her litter tray and forced Lizzie to go and get some more litter.

Boo had always been a very tidy cat. She used her litter tray without fail, never had an accident, and every time she did her business, she spent an inordinate amount of time digging not only in the tray but also scraping the lino around it, her compulsion to be thorough was so strong. It was on one such occasion that Bill and Lizzie heard the usual scratching sounds, but they were followed by an unexpected crash, and Boo shot out of the kitchen and hid under a chair. When Lizzie went to investigate, she found that the cat had tipped the whole litter tray over and dumped its contents on the floor. Worse, when she checked the cupboard, she discovered that they had used the last of the litter. It was on the list for the shopping, which, in accordance with official advice, they tried to limit to once a week and weren't due to do until tomorrow. Bill offered to clear the mess up while Lizzie went to the corner shop to get a bag of their overpriced litter. They were allowed to shop for essentials, he reasoned, and this was pretty essential.

By the time Lizzie returned, Bill had cleared up the soiled litter, a job that made him gag more than once, mopped the kitchen floor and washed and disinfected the litter tray. It was one of those occasions when washing his hands was not just government advice but an absolute necessity. He was drying his hands when Lizzie returned, bearing cat litter, bread and milk—"While they had it." Bill filled the litter tray and while he did so, Lizzie stood at the sink, washing her hands even more furiously than he had done.

"People are idiots," she pronounced as she scrubbed. "I was just paying for this when some man came and stood right behind me. I mean, *right* behind. I swear when I left the shop I heard him coughing. Didn't sound like he was coughing into a tissue either."

"Well, as long as he didn't cough on you," Bill said.

"I hope he was holding his breath, then. He might still have breathed on me. Bastard."

Bill made lunch, and they watched *Bargain Hunt* and forgot all about the man in the corner shop. They forgot about him for four days.

On the fourth day, Lizzie started with a cough. Bill had just returned from doing a major shop at the supermarket and was ready to regale his wife with a description of the queues outside and the arguments some customers were having with the security guard who was, after all, only trying to do his job, but something on Lizzie's face when he hauled the carrier bags through the living room and into the kitchen made him stop.

"I've been coughing," Lizzie said. "It's probably nothing. Maybe hay fever. I was out in the garden first thing..." She broke off and began to cough again. Bill didn't reply but went to the kitchen to fetch her a glass of water. He sat with her until the coughing subsided.

"You don't think...?" she began once she had caught her breath.

"Let's just see," Bill replied, a cold knot tightening in his stomach. "You're right. It might be nothing."

While they watched a film on the television that afternoon, Bill surreptitiously looked up the symptoms of Covid-19 on his phone, stealing glances at Lizzie and feeling sick every time she coughed. By the time they sat down to eat their evening meal, Lizzie was complaining of aches in her arms and legs. She pushed her meal away half eaten and announced that she was going to bed. Bill laid the back of his hand on her forehead.

"You're warm," he said. "Do you feel hot?"

"Just my back," Lizzie said. "I'll be fine after a good night's sleep. Don't worry."

She gave him a weak smile and went upstairs. Bill could hear how slow her footsteps were, and the knot in his stomach tightened a bit more. Once he could hear no more sounds from upstairs, he called the NHS helpline number. It took a little while to be answered, but when it was, the voice on the other end was calm, reassuring and sounded ridiculously young. They advised rest, plenty of fluids and above all isolation.

"Well, that's it," Bill said aloud to Boo, who was sitting next to him on the settee, cleaning herself. "You're stuck with us twenty-four seven for a fortnight."

At the sound of his voice, Boo stopped her ablutions and regarded him comically from beneath her raised hind leg. Then she made a small chirrup and came and sat on his lap. They remained like that for the rest of the evening, until it was time for Bill, too, to go to bed. He made Boo her supper and went off to the spare bedroom for the first time in his twenty-four years of marriage.

The following morning, after a fitful night's sleep. Bill was up early. He put the kettle on, with Boo winding in and out of his ankles until he put some food down for her. He made himself a coffee and waited. He had no intention of disturbing Lizzie until he knew she was awake and instead turned on the television, something he seldom did. There was nothing on but the news, and the news was only about the virus. He turned the television off and waited some more, a well-fed Boo curled up next to him on the settee. He had been sitting like that for nearly an hour when he heard coughing coming from upstairs. He made a mug of tea and took it up.

Lizzie sat up in bed, red in the face from coughing, her hair plastered to her forehead with sweat. She tried to speak, but it set off another bout of coughing. Bill put the tea on the bedside table, sat on the edge of the bed and placed his hand on her back (her *hot* back) until the coughing stopped again.

"How do you feel?" he asked. "Stupid question."

"Like shit," Lizzie forced a smile because they both knew how rarely she swore. "I'm burning up, and I think someone took sandpaper to my throat in the night."

"I brought you some tea," Bill said. "You should try and drink some. Do you want some water?"

"Tea," Lizzie said. Bill passed her the mug and held her hand steady as she drank. The grimace on her face as she did so betrayed how painful it was. Bill took the mug from her and put it back on the table. He held her hand and tried not to think about how laboured her breathing sounded. Eventually, she squeezed his hand and said, "I'll try and sleep a bit. You go down. We don't want you catching it, too."

"I'll be fine," Bill said. "Hard as nails, me." All the same, he released her hand and stood up.

"Love you," he said.

"Love you more," Lizzie croaked and settled back in the bed. "Now go on."

For days after, Bill would torture himself with that last *love you more*. It was something they both said and was almost a running joke, but the question which burned in his mind was *Could I? Could I have loved you more?*

The next day, Lizzie was worse, much worse. She couldn't stop coughing and was alternating between very hot and very cold, but the most worrying thing was that she was finding it difficult to breathe. It felt, she said, like someone was sitting on her chest. Bill phoned the NHS helpline straight away, and they only had one piece of advice: call an ambulance. Dazed, Bill packed a small overnight bag and helped Lizzie downstairs to wait. He sat her on the settee and held her trembling hand. Boo wandered into the room, padded over to Lizzie and sniffed her once. Lizzie stretched out a hand, but the cat shot off into the kitchen and hid under the table.

"She knows," Lizzie said between laboured breaths.

"Knows what, love?"

"She knows I'm not coming back."

"Of course you're coming back. They'll get you sorted out at the hospital and you'll be home before you know it."

"Will I, Bill? Will I really?"

"'Course you will."

Even though the paramedics, who arrived about half an hour later, wore masks covering their mouths, Bill could tell from their eyes that it wasn't good news.

"We need to get her in immediately," said one, a man whose name badge said SAUNDERS. "She's showing all the signs of Covid-19."

"Sure," Bill replied. "I'll just get her bag and my coat, and—"

"No, I'm sorry, sir," the other paramedic, a young woman interrupted. "I'm afraid you can't come."

"What do you mean I can't come?" Bill snapped. "This is my *wife*!"

"I know that, sir, and I'm very sorry. But if your wife has the virus, it's likely you have contracted it too. We can't risk you coming to the hospital if you're infected."

"So what do I do?"

"I'm afraid you'll just have to wait, sir. The hospital will contact you as soon as there's news. It's horrible, I know, but that's the way it is right now. This is the third time we've done this today."

Bill apologised and watched impotently as the paramedics brought a wheelchair and an oxygen cylinder from the ambulance. The last he saw of Lizzie was the fear in her eyes over the top of the mask administering oxygen to her failing lungs as the paramedics wheeled her out of the house and into the ambulance. He watched the ambulance leave but could not bring himself to say goodbye. He closed the door and went to sit and wait for the phone call. Boo emerged from the kitchen, jumped up on the settee next to him and curled up beside his leg, purring loudly. He rested his hand absently on her soft, warm head.

"She'll be back soon, baby," he said, tasting the lie as it left his lips.

The hospital phoned twice. The first time, a staff nurse, exhaustion slurring her voice, told him that Lizzie was in the Intensive Care Unit and they were doing all they could. When he pressed for more information, she just repeated that they would do all they could, but Bill could detect no hope. When the second call came, this time from a doctor, to tell him that Lizzie had slipped away and there had been nothing more they could do to stop it, Bill was already numb and resigned. Those were words he had played over and over again in his mind since the first call. He had not expected anything else. He put the phone down and sat there, not moving as day became night and the room grew dark. At some point, he must have wept and sometimes he probably slept a little. Boo never left his side. When the room started to grow light again, he was jolted from a doze by a tickle in his throat. He coughed once, loudly, to try and clear it, and Boo jumped down off the settee and stood in front of him staring.

"It's all right," he said. "It's just a tickle."

He stumbled to the kitchen to put the kettle on. It was always the first thing he did in the morning, and he saw no reason to change that. He had taken two mugs from the cupboard before he realised what he was doing. A tear escaped from the corner of his eye and dripped onto the worktop as he put Lizzie's mug back. The scratch in his throat would not go away, even after he drank a glass of water and he told himself that the reason his back felt warm under his shirt was that he had slept in his clothes. While the kettle boiled, he opened a pouch of cat food and put it in Boo's bowl. She would normally have rushed straight to the bowl to start lapping delicately at the gravy, but today she didn't. She sat by the French windows that led out to the small garden and looked out.

"I'm fine," Bill said. "I'll be fine." Then the cough caught in his throat, and he couldn't say any more for a while. He looked at his cat, who was still looking through the glass and refusing to come near him, and this time, he was the one who knew.

"What's going to become of you, baby girl?" he asked and had to swallow hard to get rid of the lump in his throat.

There was only one answer he could think of. He opened the French windows. Boo craned her neck to sniff the air, then, glancing once over her shoulder, took the first steps she had ever taken outside. At first, she didn't quite know what to do and looked like she might dart back inside, but Bill shut the door and watched through the glass as she jumped up onto the back wall, fixed him once with her beautiful peridot eyes, then disappeared over the wall and away.

"Goodbye, sweetheart," Bill said but didn't know whether he was talking to Lizzie or Boo.

Then he began to cough.

And cough. And cough.

BEHIND YOU

MATT TILBURY HAD quickly come to hate the weekly video conferences. It took maybe five minutes for the novelty to wear off and for him to feel like punching the screen and throwing his laptop out of the window. By the end of the first conference, he wished his colleagues were dead.

Even back in the days when things were normal and they all sat around the table in the airless, claustrophobic conference room at the office, Matt had loathed the weekly team meeting. He disliked his job and would quit in a heartbeat if he had anywhere else to go, but he was good at it. What he didn't enjoy was having to justify how good he was to a room full of kids half his age who looked and dressed like they should be at sixth-form college or playing with Lego. They were at that age where they believed they were invulnerable and that the purpose of working was to go out every Friday and Saturday night and spend their money on cocktails with absurd innuendos for names.

The difference between Matt and his colleagues was that he needed the job and they didn't. A series of wrong life choices and a messy divorce meant he had to take the job because at his age, the opportunities were few and far between, and he had to earn a wage to keep a roof over his head. Most employers apparently only needed to look at his date of birth to consign his application to the bin, and on the rare occasions he was granted an interview, he only had to look at the hipster beard on the 'area manager' conducting the interview to know he had no chance.

He had reluctantly signed up with an agency because they, at least, didn't discriminate against people over the age of forty and dealt with the few employers who still thought it made financial sense to take on temporary workers in quantity. However, the uncertainty of agency work came with a necessity to meet regular targets, and Matt was determined to do so when the alternative was more binned applications and interviews with juvenile hipsters. Of course, the children with whom he worked weren't bothered whether they met their targets or not. Where Matt had to worry about covering his rent and bills, his colleagues seemed to spend their wages on the basis that if they couldn't be seen drinking it on one of their interminable social media posts then it wasn't worth buying. Matt followed them all on their social media accounts but didn't interact with them beyond seeing their pointless photos and wishing there was a 'hate' button. If there were, he would doubtless have worn it out.

It wasn't that Matt begrudged his workmates having so few other worries that they could spend all their free time enjoying themselves (or so he told himself). No, what really rankled was that when they showed up for work on Monday morning, there was no evidence of their weekend excesses. They were as perfectly fresh, cheery and well-groomed as if they had stepped off the production line at the Ideal Identikit Employee factory. Matt, on the other hand, whose only excess was a bottle of wine on a Sunday night (which he didn't enjoy but drank to dull the anxiety of facing another week in work) came in on Monday morning feeling (and probably looking) like he had spent the weekend on a park bench with a plastic bottle of cheap cider.

None of this made the Monday team meetings any more palatable. While Matt sweated, clutching his black coffee like his life depended on it and hoping his figures were adequate, his younger colleagues lounged around without a care, sipping creations that had more in common with a dessert than a drink.

As they waited for the meeting to begin, they chatted happily about their weekends, a knowing glance or two suggesting the boasts about *Sex on the Beach* on their Facebook posts might not have referred to cocktails. They sailed through the meeting, while Matt felt the time stretch to an eternity before he could unstick himself from the plastic chair and get back to his desk. This pattern repeated Monday after Monday and showed no sign of ending, until the virus came and they were all issued with a new laptop and sent home.

Like a great many other people, Matt had not taken the situation seriously at the start. It was a newspaper scare story at a slow news time of year, like the pig flu and the bird flu, which were supposed to decimate the population and then didn't. Even if this new thing, which sounded like a bad cold, did actually turn up in Britain, it was only going to affect old or sick people. Matt was still reasonably young and healthy, so it didn't worry him.

The escalation was rapid and shocking. One day, everyone was laughing about it, the next, the instruction was issued that anyone who was able to work from home should do so. It didn't take a massive feat of mathematical prowess for Matt's firm to work out that they could save a tidy sum on their bill if their staff paid for the firm's electricity consumption instead. Cheap new laptops were issued, and Matt and his colleagues went home.

At first, it didn't affect Matt in the slightest. His job was such that as long as he had a phone and internet access, it could be done anywhere. He quite enjoyed not having to bother with shaving or worrying about what to wear. Indeed, he took a certain pleasure in taking calls from some of his least favourite clients while wearing dressing gown, T-shirt and boxer shorts. He laughed out loud at his colleagues' social media posts in which they complained about how their lives were over because they couldn't go out anymore or have their hair done or their beards trimmed. The situation made no difference to Matt's social life whatsoever; it hadn't existed before and it didn't exist now. He still had his bottle of wine on a Sunday night and sometimes opened a second one because nobody saw him on a Monday morning. For three blissful weeks, Matt did his job, submitted his figures and managed perfectly well without the Monday team meeting. In many ways, he felt like he had a lot to thank the virus for. But then the directors of the firm discovered the joys of video conferencing, and Matt's fun was over.

As far as Matt was concerned, video calls only existed in science fiction films, and he naively thought it wouldn't matter how he dressed or looked (although he did leave the dressing gown off this time). He hadn't bothered to tidy his flat, either, thinking the tiny camera on the laptop would only show his face. The first team meeting proved he had been very wrong indeed. The younger members of the team, who, it turned out, made video calls to each other all the time, all popped up in their little boxes on Matt's screen looking like they were sitting in show homes and were about to go out on the pull. Matt's little screen box showed someone with three days' worth of stubble on their chin and last night's empty wine bottle clearly visible in the background. A few barbed comments later that day on Facebook about people 'not making the effort' named no names but left their intended recipient humiliated and determined to do better next time.

For the next few weeks, a clean-shaven Matt participated in the team meeting from his tidy flat, and he grew to hate them even more than the physical meetings he had endured in the past. At least in the conference room, he could look away so he didn't have to endure those smug faces he always wanted to slap. In the video conference, they were all there, right in front of him, judging his every move, every facial expression and especially the way he delivered his sales report. And that smirk on Curtis Cummings' face, well... That was when Matt began to wish death on his teammates, followed soon after by the chance to deliver it without ever being caught.

He nearly missed it, too. Normally, the adverts that appeared while he was scrolling through Facebook simultaneously annoyed him with their frequency and bothered him with their disturbing relevance to things he had been looking at. He was vaguely aware that he could delete them if he wanted, but it seemed like too much effort, so he didn't bother. He could easily ignore the adverts for free software or apps that could do amusing things to your 'profile pic', as he never shared photos anyway. The whole idea was utterly juvenile, and despite being a bit of a dinosaur when it came to such things, he was aware of the dire warnings against downloading programmes onto your computer or your phone. One minute, you're making yourself look like a fluffy bunny rabbit, the next, someone in Romania has all your money and you're being arrested for fraud. It was a risk he wasn't prepared to take. The advert for something called VideoKill, however, was impossible to resist.

VideoKill had obviously been developed specifically to take advantage of the proliferation of video conferencing for work and social purposes. Using special effects worthy of a Hollywood blockbuster, you could make a sinister cowled figure appear behind the person of your choice and kill them in 'a variety of blood-curdling ways'. The advert showed the hooded assassin hitting a smiling young man over the head with a hammer while he was mid-conversation, followed helpfully by an 'after' image to show it was all a 'hilarious' joke and the young man was both completely unharmed and cheerfully unaware that anything had occurred. Apparently, the advert suggested, you could show your victim the clip afterwards and have a good laugh together.

Matt instantly spotted the potential for the programme, though in his case, the clips would be for his entertainment alone. He went onto his laptop, found the advert again and, after hesitating for a moment or two, accepted the Saunders Software terms and conditions (without reading them) and clicked the 'download' button. The icon appeared on his desktop, and Matt cautiously opened the programme. He was considerably reassured to find that it looked not only easy to use but also perfectly genuine and respectable. It was just a bit of fun. There was no doubt in his mind that the first person he was going to 'kill' was that self-satisfied little shit Curtis Cummings. All of a sudden, Matt couldn't wait for Monday's video conference to come round so he could try it out.

Under normal circumstances, Matt would be the first to deny that he hated anybody. There were a few people he could do without and some he really didn't like very much, but there was nobody he actively hated as such until Curtis Cummings joined the firm. It wasn't the fact that Curtis was tall and very good-looking; Matt wasn't shallow enough to be bothered about such things. At 5'11", there were plenty of people taller than he was and any number of men who were much better looking. Nor was it because Curtis got on so well with Alicia.

Alicia was one of the few people who had welcomed Matt to the team when he started. She was pretty, funny and open and genuinely seemed to enjoy Matt's company on their lunch breaks. He had no illusions that it was any more than a pleasant friendship. There was no way a girl half his age could see it as anything else, although he did enjoy the occasions when their conversations became slightly flirtatious. It might only have been a bit of a joke, but it had been a while since Matt had flirted with anybody. That all changed when Curtis joined the team and began to pay Alicia some attention, leaving Matt in no doubt that he would be spending his lunch breaks on his own in future, which pissed him off no end but not so much that he actively hated Curtis…yet. Next came the Friday-night Facebook photos of Alicia and Curtis sharing some very cosy cocktails, but even that wasn't enough to stir up feelings of hatred in Matt.

It was the sourdough bread that did it.

Matt didn't bake. He had no desire whatsoever to do so and was more than happy to leave it to the supermarkets to provide his daily bread, cakes and other baked goods. Thus he could see no reason why, suddenly, just because they weren't allowed out to play, everyone was possessed by an urge to bake bread. It wasn't even as if there was a shortage or anything. The whole world was baking bread and sharing pictures of their efforts, along with insincerely humble descriptions, and naturally, Curtis Bloody Cummings had to get in on the act. His loaf—his first attempt (he said)—was just about perfect. It was pretty obvious (to Matt, anyway) that it was the product of Tesco's ovens, but of course, the social media sycophants, including Alicia, went wild for it. The fact that Curtis's baking exploits appeared the day before Matt saw the advert for VideoKill sealed the young baker's fate. He was to be Matt's first victim.

It was ridiculously easy to do. Minutes before the Monday video conference was due to start, Matt opened the VideoKill programme and waited for his moment. He already knew when that was going to be. When each member of the team gave their report, their box expanded to fill the screen. Curtis was nothing if not predictable; he liked to wait a little while before giving his report so he could see how other people had been doing. If the first few team members had done well, Curtis would bide his time and then jump in after a couple who'd had a disappointing week so his figures would stand out. When first Deborah, then Alan reported poor sales figures, Matt could see Curtis waiting in his little box, getting ready to impress. Then Ranvir also gave a sub-par report, and it was obvious Curtis was going to go next. Matt started VideoKill, selected the gun from the murder weapons dropdown menu and, as soon as Curtis's grinning face filled the screen, clicked OK.

The result was instant. In the foreground, Curtis hammed up how he hadn't had a very good week before delivering a report that easily eclipsed the ones that had come before. In the background, a swirl of dense, black smoke cleared to reveal a figure whose face was shrouded in shadow by its cowl. The figure stood behind Curtis, who continued with his report in blissful ignorance as hooded figure raised what looked like an ancient duelling pistol and pointed it at the back of Curtis's head. Matt jumped backwards in his chair when the pistol went off and the screen was splattered with blood and gore that was so realistic he almost forgot he was watching a special effect. He hoped nobody else had observed the look of shock that must surely have registered on his face, but then all eyes would be on Perfect Curtis and not him. All the same, he was relieved when an icon appeared on the screen and asked him if he wanted to save the clip (yes) before the view returned to normal and Curtis, still very much alive, concluded his report. Matt made a mental note that next time, he would make sure he had given his report first. He was sure he was still shaking when his turn came around. The experience had been horrifying but also exhilarating, and he couldn't wait till next week when he could kill someone else.

Over the following week, Matt watched the clip of Curtis's head erupting time and time again without getting tired of it. It was incredibly convincing, which was one of the reasons he watched it so many times: trying to determine how it was done. When he was younger, Matt was fascinated by magic acts on the television. He enjoyed being amazed but enjoyed it even more when he was able to work out the secret behind the trick. This wasn't done with mirrors or wires, though. It was some kind of digital trickery Matt couldn't possibly understand, but it was entirely compelling. The only real question was, who was next?

It had to be Alan, really. Matt didn't have anything in particular against Alan; it wasn't as if he had an annoying, narcissistic personality like Curtis, or an irritating laugh like Chris, or a terrible beard like Jason (and Ben for that matter). Maybe that was why Matt selected him to be the next one to die. Alan was so devoid of any discernible personality that killing him was the only possible way of making him interesting. And interesting it certainly was when, the following Monday, Alan came to give his report, only to be cut short (from Matt's point of view) by a cowled man creeping up behind him and garrotting him until his windpipe showed through the gaping gash in his throat and the blood cascaded down over the pale-blue Asda workwear shirt he always wore. *That,* Matt thought with a mixture of disgust and fascination, *was much more interesting.* It wasn't, however, interesting enough to save when he was prompted. Even Alan's brutal murder was only interesting enough to watch once.

Even though he knew it was all a computer-generated artifice, Matt still felt a degree of guilt over what he was doing. He found it difficult to look at Curtis and Alan for what remained of the meeting and would probably have decided enough was enough, the game was over, had it not been for a remark in the team group chat later that day. The group chat had been specifically set up to exclude any of the managers, a place where the team could, if necessary, let off steam without fear of reprisal. Matt tried to stay out of it as far as possible: regardless of what it had been set up for, the chat had, before they were all consigned to their homes, been full of plans for the weekend and post-mortems of drinking sessions. There was plenty of speculation as to who was shagging whom and bitching about people in other teams.

Matt had turned off the notifications for this group because when it was in full swing, his phone was buzzing by the second. Doubtless, one of the kids on the team could have done it in an instant, but Matt could only manage to turn off *all* notifications on his phone, and there were times when he needed to know if he had received email. When he turned notifications back on again, his phone buzzed like an angry bee. Sometimes Matt was tempted and would take a quick glance at the chat, but he always regretted it when he did, so he usually left it alone.

Two days after Alan's unfortunate, imaginary demise, Matt doing a bit of housework while he waited for an email from a client, which would hopefully finally confirm an order he had been pushing for. Every time his phone buzzed, he had to leave the dishes and go into the living room where his phone was charging. It would, of course, have made more sense to bring the phone and the charger into the kitchen, but Matt wasn't glued to his phone like the kids were. For the time being, his living room doubled as his office, and that was where his phone belonged. Five times it buzzed, and every time it was another message in the group chat. Eventually, Matt's curiosity got the better of him and he had a look. Maybe somebody had heard some rumour—or possibly even some truth—about when they were going to return to work.

It couldn't have been any further from the truth. The kids were discussing what they would do on the first night out they were allowed, when all this was over, and Matt was about to close the chat when his eye was caught by a remark by Gio, one of the newer members of the team. Gio, short for Giovanni, was third generation Italian/Glaswegian. His parents owned a very successful restaurant in Glasgow city centre but had left it in the hands of their head chef and moved to Liverpool to set up another branch several years earlier. Gio was on a gap year before going to university and was working for the firm to earn enough money to go travelling. He spent all his leisure time either in the gym or out on the town. He was tanned, muscular and had an easy charm that drew people into his orbit. He was a great many things Matt should have disliked, but it was very hard to dislike him.

Amid the group's discussion of their hypothetical night out and claims of how much they were going to drink, one comment from Gio stood out.

Keep it young, yeah? Don't want him to kill the buzz.

No names were mentioned, but Matt knew it referred to him. Jesus, when he thought about some of the nights he'd had when he was younger... But maybe that was what he was these days; an old buzzkill, a drag on a night out. The thought that he had fallen so far at once saddened and enraged him. It also made up his mind. Next Monday, he would start up VideoKill one last time, and he had Gio in his sights. He spent the next few days deciding which of the methods of dispatch would be the most appropriate. In the end, he settled on the cleaver. Very fitting for Gio's culinary heritage.

At first, it looked like Gio was not going to attend the Monday conference. All the other squares appeared, and Matt felt his disappointment mounting as he scanned the faces, looking for his victim. Gio was, however, only late. His tanned, smiling face appeared just after the meeting started, and Matt barely had enough time to prepare himself because the team leader suggested that seeing as Gio had turned up late, maybe he should go first. Where others might have objected and said they weren't ready, Gio laughed, shuffled some papers and started to give his report. As he did so, Matt watched the familiar canopy of smoke appear behind Gio, slowly forming itself into the shape of the hooded assassin. The killer crept up silently and, raising a large meat cleaver, brought it down on the back of Gio's tanned, shaven head, splitting it like a ripe tomato.

The image of Gio continuing to read his report with a cleaver buried in his head and thick rivulets of blood running down his face stayed with Matt all day. But instead of feeling triumphant, it made him sad, which might have explained why Matt had the dream that night. In the dream, he was coming into the office, except that where the space would normally be flooded with fluorescent light, it was in darkness. Approaching the banks of desks where he and the rest of the team worked, he noticed someone was sitting at one of them. He drew closer and saw that it was Giovanni, hunched over a computer, the headset he used to speak on the phone clamped to his head. He looked up when he heard Matt approach.

"I might go home," he said. "I've got a bit of a headache."

Then he fell forward, his forehead hitting the desk with a crack, the handle of a meat cleaver protruding from the back of his head. Matt woke with a start; before he'd even had his first coffee of the day, he turned on his computer and uninstalled the VideoKill programme.

For the next few weeks, the Monday video conferences passed without incident. Then the government announced that the circumstances were right to re-open the country and, little by little, get its citizens back to work. Matt and the rest of the team received an email from the firm's directors that the following Monday would be the final conference by video; all necessary preparations had been made and the staff would be returning to the office the following week. Matt wasn't sure if he was disappointed or relieved.

The final video meeting had a celebratory air about it. Indeed, most of the young team members appeared wearing cardboard party hats (Matt was very glad he'd missed *that* bit of the chat), and instead of telling them to take them off, the team leader laughed and made no further comment. Many of the team seemed to be dressed ready to go on their night out, a plan that could become a reality now the bars were opening again. Even though nobody was really in a mood to deliver their sales reports, one by one they all did, until it was Matt's turn. It was then that the mood changed.

As soon as he started speaking, he became aware that the laughter and the good-natured banter that had accompanied all the other reports had stopped, and his colleagues were all staring at him. Some of them—Alicia, Jason, Miranda—were pointing at him, their eyes wide with shock. Even Curtis gasped, "What the *fuck*?"

Matt had a horrible feeling that they had all conspired to play a prank on him, but then he noticed the VideoKill icon flashing in the toolbar at the bottom of his screen, something that really shouldn't have been there.

He barely had time to register the smell of smoke that assailed his nostrils before he caught sight of movement behind him. Whirling around in his chair, he glimpsed a face beneath a cowl, a face from which red eyes burned out of skin that was rotten like decayed fruit. And then the hand fell on his shoulder. From his computer screen, the screaming began.

THIS OLD HOUSE

CLAIRE WOODS DIDN'T see the shadow behind the blinds in the upstairs window of No. 6 Thomas Road. She never thought she would see the day when she was standing outside that house again, not with a key to the front door in her hand. It wasn't the same key this time; it was a Yale key, where the last one had been a long, deadlock key, but then it wasn't the same front door, either. The old door was a mahogany-varnished wooden door, which stuck when it swelled in damp weather. It had brass fittings, coloured in places with verdigris as if a child had gone mad with a green crayon.

This new door was white uPVC with a chrome letterbox and house number. But the number was definitely 6, and there was enough left to tell straight away it was the same house. The rosemary bush, which had needed brutally cutting back every year or it would grow rampant, was gone, but underneath the window nearest the door, the stump of the yellow rose bush remained. However harsh the weather, it flowered every January. Claire's mother had told her it was because that was when Claire's brother Eddie was born, but she knew deep down it was just a coincidence. How could a rose bush know?

The bush had been pruned almost to the ground, but it would be back next January without fail. Claire wondered who would be living there by then and hoped it wouldn't be her.

It wasn't that she didn't love the house. She did, possibly rather too much. She had been born there, after all, and lived there for more of her forty-seven years than she cared to remember. Her DNA was imprinted on every brick and board, and the house was hardwired into her soul. On the wall in the main bedroom, hidden behind a wardrobe and the wallpaper, was the crude sketch of a van Eddie had drawn when he was four, and which was revealed and reminisced about every time the room was decorated.

Claire had thought she would never see that van or even the bedroom whose wall it graced again. Now she held the key to the new front door and wondered what it would take to bring herself to go in.

Her parents had bought the house in 1977, a year after they married, when they decided that if they were going to start a family, it would be in a home of their own and not in the flat they currently rented. Claire's father Chris was a history teacher and Jean, her mother, was a social worker. With decent wages coming in, they scraped together the deposit, took out a mortgage and bought No. 6 Thomas Road. It was a three-bedroom house in the middle of a 1920s terrace with a yard at the back, and they thought it was just about perfect. Eddie was born in 1978, when heavy snow made it difficult for Chris to get to the hospital to visit his wife and new son. Jean vowed then that any future babies would be home births, and true to her word, Claire Madeleine was born in the bedroom in which the wall would two years later acquire Eddie's small mural.

No. 6 Thomas Road saw years of Woods family Christmases and birthdays, arguments and laughter. Eddie and Claire left there one after another to go to university and came back with decreasing regularity during the holidays. Eddie ended up living in Newcastle while Claire returned to Liverpool, renting a flat a few miles away from Thomas Road with her partner Jayne. When that relationship ended, Claire could not afford the flat on her own and came home, moving back into the bedroom she had vacated only a few years earlier. She was there when Jean's heart, which had shown no sign of weakness, gave out suddenly one morning.

It was Claire who found her mother collapsed in the living room, her morning cup of tea soaking into the carpet. It was Claire who called the ambulance and stayed with a shell-shocked Chris while the doctors did all they could but eventually came ashen-faced into the relatives' room to announce that their best had not been good enough. It was Claire who brought her broken father back to Thomas Road and was there for him as together they organised the funeral. Eddie did what he could from a distance, but it was Claire who had to try and put Chris back together again.

In the saddest of circumstances, Claire found happiness. On a rare evening out with some colleagues, she happened to meet a beautiful, dark-haired woman with a smile that lit up the room. Her name was Sian, and within a couple of months she knew she had found someone with whom she wanted to share the rest of her life. For a while, she was torn between looking after her dad, who was slowly picking up the pieces of his life but still a shadow of the man he had been, and wanting to act on Sian's frequent suggestions that they move in together.

Nearly a year after meeting Sian, Claire moved out of Thomas Road again and set up home with the love of her life. They had been living together for a little over eighteen months when Chris, while suffering from a bout of flu, stumbled at the top of the stairs and fell headlong from top to bottom. He just about made it to the phone and called Claire, who once again had to ring for an ambulance and once again waited in the relatives' room for a doctor to bring her the news that a parent would not be coming home.

After the funeral, Claire took a couple of weeks off work and bagged up as many of her parents' possessions as she could bear to part with, weighed down by greater sadness with each run to the tip. That the entirety of her parents' lives had been reduced to a collection of *things*, and that those things were so expendable, was heart-breaking. The more it was emptied, the more the question arose in her head of exactly what was going to happen to the house itself, which now belonged to Claire and Eddie. In the end, it was Sian who said it out loud.

"Why don't we buy it?"

"I don't know. It's a big house. Maybe it's a bit big for us."

"We might need the space one day. It makes a lot of sense if you think about it. You own half of it already. We're not going to be able to buy anything with your half of the money, but we could definitely get a mortgage to buy Ed out. Do you think he'd sell?"

"Are you sure you want to do this?" Claire asked, evading Sian's question, because she knew Eddie wouldn't mind. "It's my family home. Would you want to live here?"

"We'll make it ours," Sian said, taking Claire's hand and smiling. They bought the house, but they never made it theirs.

They had plenty of plans. The house needed double glazing and central heating. It needed decorating throughout (Claire's parents might have liked the décor, but it was very dated now) and Sian preferred laminate floors to carpets. The only trouble was that every plan they had took money. They did some rough sums to see if it was worth taking a loan out to get all the work done, but right at the point when it seemed feasible, Sian was made redundant from her job. While she looked for a new one, they limped by on Claire's wage, but it left no room to take on any additional commitments. The work on the house had to wait.

All the time Sian was out of work, damp got in through the leaky old wooden window frames. When there were high winds, they occasionally found a tile from the roof lying in a jigsaw of pieces on the ground, but it was just one of many things on the list of what they would get done when Sian was working again. While she was not out every day at work, Sian did what she could to liven up the décor, cleaning and then painting the living room walls, erasing the yellow-brown nicotine stains caused by years of Claire's parents' heavy smoking. They didn't have the money to buy the best paint, so it ended up looking like an amateur job, barely any better than it was before. When, at last, Sian found another job, they agreed to wait a bit, just in case. Any plans they had to start a family were also put on hold. The house was not in a fit state for a child.

It didn't take long for the arguments to start. Sian began to express regret that they had taken on such a white elephant of a house, and Claire felt like pointing out that it was because Sian had been out of work, but she didn't. It wasn't Sian's fault and it wasn't fair.

"If it's bothering you that much, let's just sell the bloody place and downsize," she said, thinking it would shock Sian into saying something about how the house was all that was left of Claire's parents, and that they could find a way to make it work, but she didn't.

Instead, Sian smiled and said, "Yes, I think we should," and within half an hour, she was looking up the numbers for local estate agents on her phone, leaving Claire screaming inwardly and making mental apologies to her parents.

They were in luck, as it turned out. The first estate agent Sian tried, from a company called Saunders and Co., was willing to come out the next day to give an opinion on the house. Claire was in work when he came, and she spent the day uneasily waiting for a phone call from her partner. The news was as grim as she had suspected: in its current state, the house was unlikely to achieve the asking price of similar houses. Either they could spend a considerable amount of money they didn't have in getting it up to standard or put it on the market as it was and hope someone would buy it as a project. Either way, they would have to buy somewhere much smaller or take out another mortgage to make up the difference, but their savings had dwindled while Sian was out of work, and they would struggle to find a deposit. For a week or so, they didn't talk any more about it, but the house weighed ever heavier on them both, every draught a reminder. It looked like there was no way out.

Claire was torn. Part of her wanted to keep the house and try to make it work. It felt as though losing it would be an admission of failure, that she had let her parents down. She didn't really believe in an afterlife, but if there was one, she could picture her parents watching on with disappointment on their faces. It was a look she had seen many times while they were alive—disappointment over her school results, her career, her sexuality—and one she'd never seen when they looked at Eddie. She had thought that taking care of the house was the one thing she could do to make them proud, but the possibility of that was disappearing as quickly as the plaster on the bathroom ceiling was being eaten by damp.

There was another part of her, a large, insistent part that accepted the wisdom of moving on and foresaw a day when she would have to choose between the house and Sian, which wasn't a choice she ever wanted to make. As it was, Phil, the nice man from the estate agency, took the decision out of her hands.

Claire found out about Phil's call when she got home one evening to find that Sian had unexpectedly taken a few hours off work, got home before her and cooked a meal. It wasn't their usual microwave meal in front of the television, either. It was a proper *sit down at the table with candles* affair and made Claire wonder if she'd forgotten a birthday or anniversary until, over dessert, Sian had broken the news. Phil had called out of the blue that morning and asked if they were still interested in selling the house. There was, he said, a property developer who could well be interested in it.

What had Sian really excited was that this developer was selling a nearby house he had refurbished. It was smaller, and the property prices in the area in which it was located were cheaper; according to Phil, there was a good chance that Sian and Claire could offload a house in a poor state and in return get a smaller house that had been fully modernised and still have enough left to pay off the balance of their mortgage. Sian produced the sales brochure for the new house with a smile and a flourish and said that she had made an appointment for them to go and look the following evening.

Claire didn't taste the rest of the meal. The following evening, they met Phil at the other house and, as she watched Sian's grin grow with every room they looked at, Claire knew her family house was lost.

The next two months passed in a flurry of paperwork and packing, and almost before she knew it, Claire was standing in the bare, echoing hall of the house where she was born. Sian was at the new house, unpacking and arranging, and Claire had come back for a few last boxes before dropping the keys into Phil at his office. As she looked in each room for one last time, she wanted to cry, but couldn't. She felt too empty. It was only when she kissed her fingertips and brushed them against the peeling varnish of the front door she would never use again and said goodbye that the enormity of what was happening started to sink in. Tears welled up at the back of her eyes, but she swallowed them because she knew if she started crying she might not be able to stop. She got into her car and drove away without looking back.

**

Claire had to admit that the new house had a lot going for it. It was warmer, easier to maintain and she and Sian both slept better. Little by little, her walk from the train station after work became routine and she felt she was having to choke back the word 'home' when referring to the old house less often. She didn't want to see the progress being made on the renovation of her old house and tried very hard to stay away but couldn't quite manage it. Whenever she was in the area, her car seemed to turn automatically down Thomas Road and drive past, enabling Claire to see the mountains of masonry and timber accumulated in the skip that seemed to be permanently outside. New double-glazed windows had been installed (white, which she didn't really think suited the house) and a new door (which she definitely didn't like). She tried to observe it all with a dispassionate eye, as if it were someone else's house, which, of course, it was.

The day she saw the For Sale sign go up outside hit her like a steamroller. She drove back to the new house—back home—feeling sadder than she had thought possible. Sian tried to get out of her what was wrong, but she had difficulty putting it into words and pretended it was nothing. When they were in bed that night, she could hold it in no longer and confessed. She thought Sian might make light of it, that she might even be cross, but she didn't. She just held her and stroked her hair and said, "Don't you see? Someone else is going to love that house now. It's going to be a part of their story, just like it was part of yours. It's a good thing."

Claire smiled, almost against her will, and realised that she agreed.

"Do you know what I'm going to do? When someone buys it and moves in, I'm going to put a card through the door to tell them who I am and what the house meant to me and wish them well."

"That," Sian said, "would be a beautiful thing to do."

Claire went to sleep that night feeling more at peace than she had for a long time.

She didn't go near the house for a month. She knew it would sell quickly—it was a good house in a desirable area. She had written the card, wording it carefully and wavering about whether even to sign it (she did, and gave her mobile number) and kept it in the glove compartment of her car. She wanted to give it long enough for someone to move into the house but not too long, and a month seemed about right.

It was with some trepidation that she pulled into Thomas Road and saw that the For Sale board had indeed gone and the house appeared to be inhabited. There was a car she had never seen before outside and blinds up in the new windows, replacing the faded, worn curtains she and Sian had put up with for years. What's more, there was a light on upstairs in the room where she had been born. Without giving herself a chance to hesitate and leaving the engine running, she jumped out of the car and pushed the card through the letterbox. Not wanting to be observed, she hurried back to her car and drove away, thinking it would be the last she heard of No. 6 Thomas Road, and for nearly two years, it was.

It was mostly a happy time. Claire and Sian got on with their lives and got on with each other. They (Sian mostly) decorated and furnished the house and made it their own. They worked, took occasional holidays, went out with friends and sometimes entertained them in their house. They celebrated first one Christmas, with the thrill of buying all new decorations and creating new routines and traditions, and then a second. Any plans for children were still on hold, but their family did expand with the acquisition of a cat called Eliot. Claire had considered getting a dog, but Sian reasoned that a kitten would be marginally less destructive than a puppy, and so they adopted Eliot from a local rescue centre. Claire wondered from time to time when Sian would stop protecting the house and relax and live in it; she sometimes thought that if they had bought new furniture instead of second-hand, Sian would probably have kept the cellophane on the seats. But Sian was happy, and most of the time, so was Claire.

Then, towards the end of summer, when Claire and Sian had a rare midweek day off together, the telephone call came.

Sian was pottering about outside in the small garden and Claire was catching up with some reading. The fact that it was a peaceful day made it all the more startling when Claire's mobile suddenly rang. She glanced at the number on the screen—it was a local number but not one she recognised—and she hesitated briefly before answering. She was greeted by a male voice.

"Is this Ms.—er—Woods?" the voice asked. "Claire Woods?"

"Yes, it is," Claire replied. "Who's this?"

"I'm sorry to ring out of the blue. My name is Simon Kane, from Morton Beattie solicitors. I'm hoping you can help me. As I said, I'm sorry to call you like this, but we have a slightly unusual situation and it seems to concern you."

"Go on," Claire said, curious but apprehensive.

"Can I ask if you know a Mr. John Shellbourne?"

"I don't think so," Claire replied, though there was a nagging feeling at the back of her mind that she had heard the name somewhere before.

"In that case, might I ask if you are familiar with a house in Thomas Road? Number six?"

"Yes, I am." A queasy feeling invaded Claire's stomach. "I used to own it. Why?"

"This is where is gets a bit unusual," Kane said. "It appears that Mr. Shellbourne bought the house from you. Does that ring any bells?"

Of course. That was where she had seen the name before. A half-registered, barely relevant name on a vast amount of paperwork.

"If you say so," Claire said. "It was a couple of years ago now."

"I see that. Here's the thing, Ms. Woods—sorry, can I call you Claire?"

"If you like."

"Thank you. Here's the thing, Claire. We are John Shellbourne's solicitors, although I see he used another company in the purchase of the house. Mr. Shellbourne passed away a month or so ago, and we are charged with executing his estate."

"I'm sorry," Claire said automatically, even though she hadn't known John Shellbourne and, from the sound of it, neither had this Simon Kane.

"It appears to have been quite sudden from all accounts, which makes what we found in the will more unusual. Mr. Shellbourne made his will a little over six months ago—we're not sure if it was his first, or a new one—but either way, you are a beneficiary in his will. He only seemed to have your mobile phone number, so I'm glad you haven't changed it or we might never have found you. The fact of the matter is that Mr. Shellbourne left you quite a large bequest. He left you the house, Claire. You are now the owner of number six Thomas Road again."

***

Claire didn't tell Sian. She intended to because one way or another, they kept no secrets from each other, but she needed time to process the information. If nothing else, it raised two very big questions: what were they going to do with two houses, and, more importantly, could she bring herself to sell that house again? She knew she couldn't decide before she'd seen the house again, but she had to go alone. If she told Sian, there was no way that would happen. So, when Sian came back in from the garden, Claire did her best to pretend nothing had happened.

The next day, she booked another annual-leave day for later in the week, using an uncharacteristic lie of a sick relative, and made an appointment to see Simon Kane to collect the keys. Two days later, and with Sian still none the wiser, she was standing outside No. 6 Thomas Road, wondering whether she had the courage to go inside. She wished she hadn't asked Kane the question that had been at the forefront of her mind since his initial phone call. She wished she hadn't asked what happened to John Shellbourne.

As soon as she opened the door to the small porch, she would see the staircase down which John Shellbourne had fallen after, the assumption was, catching his foot in his dressing gown. She hoped someone had cleaned the newel post at the bottom of the stairs where he had hit his head, causing the brain injury from which he never recovered. Claire had placed her hand on the ball at the top of that post so many times, yet she wasn't sure she ever wanted to touch it again. In the end, there was one factor that made her open the door and go in; she didn't want any of her old neighbours to see her standing there and start asking difficult questions about why she was back, not until she was ready to answer them.

Once through the front door, she noticed the first change: the frosted glass in the porch door had been replaced with plain glass. This made her sad straight away. She used to love running her fingers over that glass, feeling the pattern like small waves beneath her fingertips. The plain glass had no character. She gave herself a stern talking-to, realising that she probably wasn't going to like any of the changes that had been made to the house—the pale-grey paint on the porch walls might have been fashionable but had no warmth—and if she got upset by every change, she would never be able to look around properly. She took a deep breath and opened the porch door.

In some ways, the hall looked much the same, except that all the doors had been replaced and the walls had been stripped of the embossed wallpaper that had been painted so many times over the years. Everywhere had been painted the same utilitarian grey as the porch, and Claire had to admit it looked cleaner and fresher than it had when she'd left. The hall carpet, which Sian had hated, was gone and replaced with laminate flooring. Claire was not used to hearing the sound of her own footsteps in this hall. The emptiness of the house made them echo, and she very nearly removed her shoes so she could creep around until she remembered that there was no one to hear.

The doors to the back living room and front room were closed; only the kitchen door was open. From where she stood, Claire could see different worktops and what looked like stone tiles on the floor, although it was probably a vinyl flooring designed to give that effect, but she wasn't ready to look in the downstairs rooms yet. Careful not to touch the newel post (even though it had been cleaned), she went upstairs instead.

The bathroom at the top of the stairs was familiar yet different. The toilet, sink and bath were all in the same place, but they were white rather than the blue suite Claire's parents had installed back when coloured bathroom suites were fashionable. The most noticeable thing was that the sink had a selection of men's toiletries on it, something which had not been the case since she had thrown the remnants of her father's possessions away. John Shellbourne had obviously not been overly concerned with grooming, as the soap and shaving foam were supermarket own brands.

Claire closed the bathroom door, and as she crossed the landing to look in the first of the spare bedrooms, she felt a chill in the air. She hadn't felt it when she first came into the house. She was used to it being cold when she lived there; the draught seeped in through most of the windows, and the only sources of heat were an ancient gas fire in the living room, which should have been condemned years ago, and a succession of fan heaters and radiators in the bedrooms. They were spoiled now by central heating and windows that didn't let the heat out.

The chill she felt as she crossed the landing was different from the chill all houses acquire when they've been empty for a while. It ran up her spine and went bone deep, and she was torn between curiosity and an urge to get out of the house as quickly as possible and go somewhere warm. Curiosity won. One of the spare bedrooms was completely empty, never used. Whether John Shellbourne had a purpose in mind for it was something nobody would ever know now, but for now, apart from clean, painted walls and a new, rather dull carpet, there was nothing to see.

The other spare bedroom was much the same, apart from a pile of neatly stacked boxes at one end. Clearly, Shellbourne had brought a lot of stuff with him—books or DVDs, maybe—which he had thought he wanted to keep but hadn't missed enough to unpack yet. Claire thought about having a look in the boxes, but it felt too intrusive, too personal. It would have to be dealt with one day, but not today. She closed the door on them and crossed the landing again to the front bedroom, the main bedroom, the one in which she had been born and in which first her parents and then she and Sian had slept. If a pile of boxes felt intrusive, this felt more so. She was about to go into John Shellbourne's most private space and wasn't sure she was ready for what she would find there. She took a deep breath and opened the door.

Shellbourne had clearly lived alone. Claire could tell as soon as she opened the door. The room had a definite male smell about it. It was not unpleasant, but unlike when she and Sian had shared this room and the air was heavy with mingled perfumes and hairspray, now it smelled of clothes and the faint odour of an aftershave she couldn't identify. The room was tidier than she had expected. There were a few items of clothing on the floor, but everything else was so neat Claire envisaged that even the pullover and pair of trousers would have been tidied away had their owner not met with his unfortunate accident.

There was another thing about the room that struck her as odd. Most of the wardrobes were tight against the wall, but one had been pulled away, leaving a gap of about a foot behind it. Claire didn't need to look to tell which wall it was but did so anyway. Behind the wardrobe, the wallpaper had peeled away and lay in a soggy lump on the floor. Evidently, not all the damp had been cured, but it was odd that the only place still affected was this one. The only piece of wallpaper to peel away from the wall exposed Eddie's naïve drawing of a van. The sight of it brought a lump to her throat, and she had to look away. It was too much, and she turned to leave the room, but then she heard something that made her freeze. She could have sworn she heard someone speak. She listened intently for a moment, wondering if she had imagined it, if she had caught a stray sound from a radio or television next door, but then she heard it again, more distinct this time.

"*She's up there.*"

It was a male voice, and it came from downstairs. She was not alone in the house. She quickly looked around the bedroom to see if she could spot something—anything—she could use as a weapon, but there was nothing. She quickly decided that her best bet was to sneak down the stairs and try to get out of the front door before anyone saw her. Once outside, she could call the police.

The landing was darker when she left the bedroom that it had been when she went in. It looked for all the world as though dusk had fallen, but she didn't need to look at her watch to know it wasn't even midday yet. It was probably about to rain, which was all she needed. At the top of the stairs, she reached out a hand to steady herself and was surprised to feel the ridges of the embossed wallpaper, something she had felt without even registering it every time she had gone downstairs for so many years. Now it felt wrong. It couldn't be there. She had seen the smooth, grey walls on her way up.

She crept down the stairs, touching the wall over and over again, sure she must be mistaken, but she felt the pattern every time. Impossible as it seemed, she had made no mistake; the old wallpaper was there. Then her feet touched the floor at the bottom of the stairs and it yielded beneath her feet— carpet not laminate—and she suddenly found it difficult to move, frozen in confusion. The voice spoke again, and this time she knew it was coming from the living room.

"She's here."

Every nerve in her body screamed at her to go straight out of the front door, but it was as if her feet no longer belonged to her, impelling her across the carpet, her arm lifting as if being pulled by strings to reach out and take hold of the living room door handle, wooden like it used to be, not metal like the uniform new doors in the rest of the house. She smelled the room before she had even opened the door. It had odours of damp and cigarettes and something else, something rotten she couldn't identify. She turned the handle and pushed the door open.

The foetid air hit her and made her want to gag, a stench like meat left to rot in hot weather, and the smoke stung her eyes. She blinked the tears away and stared through the haze into the room, her brain struggling to make sense of what it was seeing. The hideous cottage suite was one of the first things to go to the tip when she and Sian had moved in, yet even though she could only see the back of one of the armchairs, it was clearly there. The wallpaper was the anaglypta that Sian had painted over, but it was sagging under the weight of mould and damp.

Slate-grey smoke drifted up from the chair's occupant—a sight Claire had seen time and time again. She stepped into the room and looked to her right, knowing she would see the matching chair. The sight of who—what—was sitting in the chair made her drop to her knees and vomit onto the sodden carpet. It was in the shape of a woman, but the flesh was rotting away from the bones, held together by soil and sinew and tattered skin. The smoke from the cigarette clamped between what was left of this thing's teeth was leaking out through gaps in the flesh and polluting the air. It turned its head and looked at Claire.

"Welcome home," her mother said. "It's about time."

THE CALL

I WAS OUT IN my garden, tending to the roses, when the call came. The roses didn't actually need much attention, just a small amount of deadheading. Most of the time, they managed to look after themselves and still remain beautiful, which was one of the reasons I was so fond of them.

I never liked gardening until I came here. I always viewed it as a chore, something that intruded on my weekend leisure time. Because Angie was in charge of the creative side of things, I was responsible for the drudgery—the mowing, the digging, and the heavy lifting. Much as I enjoy sitting out in the garden, I prefer to relax with a cold beer because I want to, not because I need to sit down after mowing the grass for an hour in the sun. When Angie finally came and joined me, she would look around with the satisfied grin of someone who knew the garden looked so nice because of her artistry...and nothing to do with my hard work. The garden was her creation; I did the donkeywork to make it happen but had no say in its design.

Since moving to the cottage and leaving Angie to her own garden, I've become much more interested in the colours and shapes that form the view from my window. I have plenty of time on my hands these days and not many demands on it. Wandering around in my garden fills some of that time and helps me relax, not that I have much to worry about anymore, with no work and no bills. I'm free to do what I want, and when at one time I would have found that boring, since I left Angie behind and came here,

I have no problem occupying my hours. I'm not quite sure why that should be, but I enjoy it as much as I can. If I've learned one thing, it is that life can change very quickly and unexpectedly, and it is wise to appreciate what you have.

I try to appreciate the peace and tranquillity that surround me, which is why any calls feel like an intolerable intrusion, and when I heard the phone ringing in the cottage, my first instinct was to ignore it. I successfully shut the sound out and concentrated instead on the song of the birds in the trees surrounding the garden. After a while, the ringing stopped, and I hoped that would be the end of it, but after a few minutes, it started again. Whoever it was had no intention of going away, so I decided it would be better to answer it and get rid of them. Reluctantly, I went back into the cottage.

"I'm busy," I said by way of a greeting.

"No, you're not," said the voice on the other end. "You're never busy."

"Mel. I might have known."

"Well, who else was it going to be? You don't get junk calls anymore."

Mel made it very hard to be rude. She was one of Angie's best friends and had become one of mine too. She was bubbly and easy-going, and I had liked her from the moment Angie introduced us. Although around the same age, she had been Angie's line manager at work, but they had really hit it off, and when Angie moved jobs, it became far easier to remain friends. She was single (most of the time) but didn't seem to feel any awkwardness about being friends with a couple. When I left Angie, she stayed in touch, although she was about the only one of our friends who did.

"How have you been?" she asked.

"Much the same. Nothing much changes here. What about you?"

"Can't complain. Work's okay. Life's okay. I haven't got much to report, really, except..."

"Except?"

"I'm not really sure how to tell you this. I wasn't sure whether to tell you at all."

"Well, you've kind of started now. You'd probably better carry on."

"I don't want to hurt your feelings..."

"It's all right, Mel. I think my feelings are a bit beyond being hurt now. It's Angie, isn't it? Is she okay?"

"She's fine, Mike. She's more than fine, in fact. She's...she's been seeing someone. For a while now. I didn't want to tell you if it wasn't serious because there wouldn't have been much point, but now..."

"Now it *is* serious?"

"It certainly looks like it."

"Is it anyone I know?"

"No. She met him through work. He's an accountant. His name's Tim."

"Tim."

"Yes."

"An accountant."

"Chartered, I believe."

I fell silent while I digested the news. A chartered accountant called Tim. She was always a thrill seeker, my Angie.

"Mike? Are you still there? Are you okay?"

"Yes, I am. I'm just taking it in."

"Are you upset?"

"Surprisingly, no," I told her and meant it. "I'm made up for her, Mel, really I am. She shouldn't be on her own. She always had a lot of love to give. So it's really serious, is it?"

"Well, that's kind of why I had to tell you. They're engaged."

"Engaged? Wow. I see what you mean. That's serious, right enough. Listen, when you see her, tell her I wish her every happiness in the world. Really. She deserves it."

"I don't think she's ready to hear that."

"How come?"

"For a start, she doesn't know I talk to you."

"What? Have you never said?"

"No. It's never the right time. It would have seemed a bit weird, don't you think?"

"Yes, I suppose it would. But we were always such good friends, Mel. I think Angie would be okay with you talking to me. Mind you, she did ask me once if I fancied you. Did you know that?"

"No! Did she? When was that?"

"Ages ago. It was one night we'd all been out and she'd had a few. She wasn't being nasty or anything, just curious."

"I'm curious now. What did you say?"

"I denied everything, of course. What else could I say?"

Mel laughed on the other end of the phone, a deep, hearty, genuine laugh. I missed that laugh.

"Anyway, things are different now," she said, serious again. "She still talks about you, and I can see it still hurts. I just thought it was best not to mention it."

"It'll be two years next month, Mel. It's not like I only left her yesterday."

"I know, Mike. But it was always a bit difficult to know how to start."

"Why? Doesn't she know you're...you know..."

"A medium? No, Mike, no one does. It's not something I broadcast. You can see my problem, though. Put yourself in my shoes. 'Hey, Angie, guess what? I've been talking to your dead husband. He's thrilled for you.' She'd have me locked up."

"Good point. Thanks for letting me know, though, Mel. I honestly really do appreciate it. And I am really happy for her. Even if she is marrying someone called Tim. You did the right thing."

"As long as you're sure."

"I am. Take care, Mel."

"You too, Mike."

I stood looking at the phone for quite some time after I hung up. I didn't know how to feel. I always knew this day would come, and of course I didn't want Angie to stay single forever. Black never suited her anyway; she was better suited to colours, always wearing reds and oranges and browns, like autumn. I smiled and wandered back into the garden. I didn't hurry. I had all the time in the world. It's not like I had anywhere better to be.

THAT DAMN SONG

BILLY MATHER WISHED he'd never written that damn song. He used to only hate it at Christmas; now he hated it all the time. Back in the good old days when he only despised the song for a month (Or maybe six weeks) a year, it followed him everywhere. He would be in a supermarket, or just about any shop, and before he knew where he was, there would be *those* sleigh bells, and *that* chord sequence, and it would kick off. It seemed to be playing in every bar or restaurant he went in and ruined many a good meal or drinking session.

He could tell by the order of the tracks on most Christmas compilation albums, for example, if Wizzard followed Paul McCartney, when it was time to go because the next track would start with those bastard sleigh bells and that sequence, and he liked to be out of the place before that happened. One Christmas, he tried to avoid it by going abroad, but even in Dubai there was no escape. He was in the lift going up to his room and a tinny Muzak version of the song came on, forcing him to vacate the lift and take the stairs the rest of the way. It was twelve bloody floors. The trouble was, when you'd written a song that got to number one at Christmas, come the festive season, the chances were you'd hear it everywhere.

It wasn't even supposed to be a Christmas song. Billy had been a moderately successful singer/songwriter in his own right, and while his singles didn't trouble the upper reaches of the charts, his two albums did well. The second one even earned him a silver disc, which he kept on the wall until it became too much of a pain to keep dusting it, at which point it was thrown in the loft, where, as far as he knew, it still resided. He had a loyal and enthusiastic fan base, albeit one which had stubbornly refused to change his life by doing anything useful, like, for example, making him large amounts of money. He made a living and that was it. His manager, Steve Hammond, got him enough gigs to keep him busy but spent more time promoting his label-mate, Jon Craze. Billy wasn't altogether surprised. When you had an international superstar like Jon Craze on your books, it was likely to take up most of your time and energy and wouldn't leave a lot of room in your schedule for a guy who wrote and sang intelligent songs about the state of the world but never reached the top twenty.

Billy was laying down some tracks for his third album on the fateful day when Steve arrived at the studio and asked the question that would change his life forever.

"I don't suppose...you've got any Christmas songs."

"Steve, you've heard my albums. Is there anything remotely like a Christmas song on them?"

"No, I guess not."

"Well, there's your answer, then."

"Pity. Jon's looking for a Christmas song. Everyone's done one. Elton, Lennon, even Shakin' fucking Stevens, and they're all massive. Royalties every year without fail. It would be a nice little earner for whoever wrote one for Jon. Jona Lewie's set for life and his wasn't even meant to be a Christmas song. Still, if you haven't, you haven't."

Steve then proceeded to do that thing he did, the thing that drove Billy mad; he mooched. He hung around the studio, picking things up and looking at them without any real interest in whatever was in his hand. It served no purpose apart from getting right on Billy's nerves. Steve couldn't simply say what he had to say and then go, he had to bloody mooch. On this occasion, however, the mooching did in fact serve an unexpected purpose. He suddenly stopped what he was doing and turned to Billy, a big grin on his face.

"What's this tune? It's terrific."

"It's one of the cuts for the new album. It's called 'You're Not on My Side.'"

"It's really catchy. Not like your other stuff. I mean, don't get me wrong, you've written loads of great songs, but they're not that easy to, you know, join in with. This one's got a real hook. Hey, maybe if you put some sleigh bells on it…"

"It's not a Christmas song, Steve. It's about the miners' strike, for God's sake."

"Yes, but it needn't be. Just change the words. Put the sleigh bells on it and maybe some little kids singing. It's got Christmas number one written all over it."

"Not by me, it hasn't. I told you, Steve, I don't do Christmas songs. People don't expect things like that from me."

"But you wouldn't be singing it."

"Jon would." Billy wasn't sure if that was better or worse.

"It makes sense," Steve said. "I could see if he'd write the lyrics if you want. If you don't mind splitting the royalties, that is."

Billy sighed. Steve had him over a barrel, and the barrel was full of mulled wine and covered in holly.

"Leave it with me," he said and regretted it immediately because he had already had an idea. Put a few minor chords in here and there, change the title to 'You're Not *by* My Side' and make it about being separated from your loved one at Christmas. A bit of misery didn't do Elvis any harm when he whinged on about having a 'Blue Christmas', and Mud had done very well with 'Lonely This Christmas'. He'd make it shamelessly sentimental, a real heartstring-tugger, and see how Craze got on with that. Billy doubted his label-mate had the emotional range.

He was wrong.

Jon Craze adored the song when he heard it and astonished everyone by singing it straight and actually doing a great job. Steve made sure it was released in exactly the right week to catch the Christmas market, and it stormed straight up the charts, hitting number one in early December, and there it stayed until the middle of January. That Christmas, it could be heard pretty much everywhere. It was on *Top of the Pops* every week and on the Christmas Day edition, of course. It was all over the radio, and Jon Craze, dressed in a red suit and shades, like a cross between Orbison and Santa, was on every TV show going.

That was just the start. It was re-released the following year and nearly made it to number one again. For the next thirty years, it was on every Christmas compilation and was covered by dozens of other artists. Every year, a progressively older Jon Craze, who had not had a hit of quite that magnitude again, was wheeled out onto every show that would have him, still dressed in the red suit, although it had been let out a few times since its original appearance. The royalties afforded Billy Mather a lifestyle that recording his own songs would never have given him and enabled him to concentrate on writing and singing whatever he wanted without ever having to worry about selling another album or concert ticket.

That, of course, is what would have happened in an ideal world, but the world is less than ideal, and so was Billy Mather's life. He had, up until then, never measured success by sales figures. Only very rare artists had continued success with serious material, the public generally preferring their records to be froth about love and things like that. There were plenty of superb songwriters singing songs of protest or rebellion, but usually only for rather more select audiences; not everyone could be Dylan.

The success of 'You're Not by My Side' made Billy think, though. He had written a platinum-selling song, so surely he deserved to be more widely appreciated than he was. The trouble was, Steve didn't seem to agree and carried on booking him the same gigs and promoting his records in the same niche way. Frustrated, after nearly twenty years together, he sacked Steve Hammond and hired the up-and-coming Jamie Walcott as his new manager. Jamie promised him the world and even seemed to mean it when the first thing he did was get Billy an interview in the *NME*. Billy was quite excited about this until the article came out and it was more along the lines of a 'Where Are They Now?' retrospective. After that, Jamie delivered about as much as Steve had, and Billy Mather remained famous to exactly the same people as he had been famous to before.

The frustration Billy felt, coupled with the seasonal ubiquity of the song he now bitterly resented but earned him more money than he knew how to spend, had encouraged him to acquire a serious alcohol and cocaine problem, and he was getting through his royalties almost as quickly as he could earn them. He was touring almost constantly, mainly for something to do, and although there had been many people sharing his bed over the years, nobody had stayed long.

The drink and the drugs staved off the boredom and most of the time stopped him thinking about what could have been. He spent the Christmas period every year drinking himself into oblivion, and more snow went up his nose than settled on the ground. Every now and then, he tried to get his life back on track and booked himself into a rehab centre to dry out. His good intentions lasted until the first time 'You're Not by My Side' was played, usually about mid-November, and then he sought out the nearest bar that didn't play music or had a chat with one of the dealers who had been missing his business.

Ironically, it was while Billy was on one of his rehab holidays that the news broke about Jon Craze.

Craze had, like many of his contemporaries, enjoyed a roller coaster of a career. He had been in and out of fashion since the late

70s and had hit all the milestones: he had been hugely popular, hugely derided, ironically retro and seriously retro. He had done the album collaborating with Eno and the big band album of songs from the Great American Songbook. He hadn't had a number one hit for decades but was somehow never out of the press. Then, suddenly, thanks to the despicable actions of several public figures whose careers had peaked around the time Craze's took off, the lives of everyone who enjoyed fame around that time and was still alive (and indeed some who weren't) came under scrutiny. Some people who thought they had got away with truly atrocious behaviour suddenly discovered they could no longer run and the law caught up with them. When the storm reached its peak, accusations were made on near enough a daily basis against name after name, many of whom deserved it and some of whom did not. One of the names that hit the press with a bang was Jon Craze.

It was probably a mistake for Craze to bring out his autobiography during a period when everyone's memory of the past was being questioned. There was nothing particularly contentious in the book; indeed, anyone who read it (and plenty did) would have recognised that the picture it painted of the 1970s had been somewhat sanitised. What brought Jon Craze back into the headlines was the companion book, the autobiography of Jackie Giles, Jon Craze's first wife. Jackie was a model whose face was everywhere in the early and mid-70s, and her wedding to Craze in 1976 was one of the most photographed events of the decade. They lasted eight years before splitting in 1984. Jon Craze married his second wife, Dawn, in 1986 and had been married to her ever since. Jackie Giles more or less disappeared from view until Craze wrote his life story, which dealt with his and Jackie's marriage in a couple of short chapters, and a smart publisher decided that a rather fuller version, told from Jackie's point of view, might be just as much of a bestseller.

Jackie's version told of a tempestuous relationship and Jon's many affairs. It also told of his drunken rages and the furious rows that ended their marriage. She was particularly scathing about the Christmas song that had made Craze a massive star. "He might have had a hit with 'You're Not by My Side', but he was *never* by my side," she said in one interview, a quote which then appeared just about everywhere. The book outsold Craze's own, and although he furiously denied all the allegations and threatened libel action, the public's tolerance for the misdeeds of their former heroes was at an all-time low; Jon Craze's career was all but finished. 'You're Not by My Side' was dropped from every Christmas compilation CD, and Billy Mather finally got his wish. He never had to listen to that damn song again.

Jackie Giles's autobiography didn't just kill off her ex-husband's career, though. With that song no longer being played anywhere, Billy's songwriting royalties dried up at a time when it was very much too late for him to regret frittering them away over the years. Billy was left back where he was before he wrote the song; virtually unknown and almost completely broke. He hated that song even more than he had when it was everywhere now that it was not being played at all.

On Christmas Eve, newly out of rehab and starting to get to work on his journey back again, Billy sat hunched over his second-to-last pint (he had just about enough money left for one more) and tried to decide if his Christmas present to himself this year should be killing himself or killing Jon Craze. Killing himself would be easier, but killing Craze, while more difficult since it involved finding the man and getting close enough to do the deed, would probably be more satisfying. It was a difficult decision, albeit a hypothetical one, seeing as he was fairly sure he didn't have the courage to do either. Paul McCartney came on the festive soundtrack in the pub, and Billy sneered every time Macca warbled the word 'wonderful'.

BOB STONE

When that song finished and Roy Wood took over the Yuletide platitudes, Billy felt the old instincts to get up and leave start to take over, but he stuck it out as the children's choir and sleigh bells faded out and a terrible cover version of 'Fairytale of New York' with the dodgy words butchered out came on instead of the track that would normally have been there. Billy drained his pint and ordered another one. As he did so, he became aware of a man sitting on the next stool, a man who was probably middle-aged, judging by the greying hair at his temples, and who had managed to arrive and sit down before Billy had even realised he was there. He was staring at Billy intently.

"Excuse me," he said. "But aren't you Billy Mather?"

"Used to be. I'm not sure what I am now."

"Oh, man! This is awesome! I'm such a big fan. I saw you first at Eric's in '81, and I've followed you since."

"That's...er... That's good to hear. Thank you."

"So are you working on anything right now? It's been a while since you had anything new out."

"Four years," Billy said bitterly. "Yeah, I am. Got a few things lined up. I'm hoping to drop a new album next year and..." He stopped and took a long pull on his new pint. "No. Not a bloody thing."

"Now that's a shame. You should be better known, really you should. I always thought it was criminal that only that terrible Christmas song did anything for you. And that Jon Craze. What a shit."

"Tell me about it. That's why I'm here with nowhere else to go."

"Let me get you another pint," the man said. "There's something interesting you should know."

***

196

Billy still had the words of a half-remembered conversation running through his head as he walked across the city to another bar. Snow had begun to fall, not heavy enough to stick but just enough to make the pavement treacherous underfoot, but he went as quickly as he could. There was someone in the other bar he had to see and something he had to do, and time was of the essence. He located the bar in a side street he had never noticed before and expected, when he opened the door, to find it full of people. It wasn't. It was virtually empty. Billy felt momentarily sad for the bar's owners. If this was their Christmas Eve trade, then they would be lucky still to be there in the New Year. Perched on a stool at the bar, much as Billy had been earlier, and staring into a whisky as if all the answers could be found within, was Jon Craze, exactly as the stranger had told him. From the way Craze's shoulders sagged, Billy could see that the man was teetering on the brink of something—madness, oblivion maybe—and it wouldn't take much of a push to send him over the edge. Billy had come here to push. He took up the stool next to Craze and ordered a pint, paying with money he didn't remember having in his pocket.

"Can I get you one, Jon?"

Craze turned his head and looked at Billy through red-rimmed, bleary eyes.

"Billy Mather." Judging by way he slurred the words, he was a way into a major session. "I'll have a drink with you. Least I can do."

Billy indicated to the barman to refill Craze's glass. The barman gave him a look conveying *Are you sure that's a good idea?* Billy nodded, so the barman poured.

"What are you doing, Jon?" Billy asked. "It's Christmas Eve. Shouldn't you be at home?"

"I know it's bloody Christmas Eve. I'm Mr. Christmas, remember?" He laughed bitterly and without humour. "And

I haven't got a home anymore. Dawn doesn't want me there, and the kids don't want to know."

"I'm sure that isn't true."

"The publishers sent her a copy, you know. Ahead of publication. They didn't send it to me. They sent it to her. Bastards. They wanted to make sure she saw it."

"Does she believe it?"

"Of course she does. She already knew. I told her years ago. She married me knowing about it. She nearly didn't marry me. She walked out for a week—to think, she said. I don't know why she ended up taking a chance on me. She should have kept walking."

"You mean it's all true? What Jackie said about you?"

"Every word. I used to drink far too much, and we used to fight a lot. I wasn't a good person back then. I was a piece of shit and I'll never stop being ashamed of it. Dawn changed me. She told me if I carried on drinking, she'd leave straight away, and I believed her. This is the first time I've been pissed in thirty-two years."

"Then maybe you should stop."

"What for? I'm finished. I'm going to have a few more drinks and then I'm going for a swim in the Mersey. The sort of swim you don't come back from."

"Why? Jon, you can't do that!"

"I can. And I will. Thing is, Billy, nothing revives a career in this business like death. It gets rid of bad reputations and sells a shitload of records. Look at Lennon. Who remembers he wasn't squeaky clean? It'll keep Dawn for life. It's all I can do for her now."

This is it, Billy thought, *this is the bit where you push. You can kill him without lifting a finger.* As he thought them, the words felt alien in his head, as if they were not his words but someone else's, and he knew he couldn't do it.

"You need to fight this," he said. "You can't fight it if you're dead."

"Fight it? What do you mean, fight it? I can't fight it, Billy, because it's true."

"I mean you have to fight for Dawn. She's stuck by you all these years. Now you've got to prove you were worth it."

"How can I do that? I'm *not* worth it."

"Then *be* worth it. Tell the world what you've just told me. Apologise. Settle as much money on Jackie as she wants and— I don't know—set up a charity or something. If you've got to spend the rest of your life atoning for this, then do it and do it like a grown-up. You really think Dawn will ever forgive you if you take the coward's way out?"

Billy got up and drained the last of his pint.

"Think it over, Jon," he said. "Go home and give your wife the best Christmas she's ever had and think about it. If you still want to top yourself, do it in the New Year. Don't give her this to remember every year."

He went to leave but then stopped as an idea struck him.

"I think you need to record another version of that song. I've still got your email. I'm going to send you over some new lyrics. How does 'You're *Still* by My Side' sound?"

"It sounds better than that other damn song," Craze said. "And thanks, Billy. I'll see you straight."

"See that you do. I'm seriously skint."

With that, Billy walked out of the pub and into the night.

Outside, the air was cold and damp with sleet. It wasn't going to be a white Christmas this year. Over the road, he could see a figure standing in a doorway, a middle-aged man with greying hair. Billy aimed a one-fingered salute at him.

"Happy Christmas," he said, and went home to write.

THE AUTHOR'S TALE
(PART 2)

I HAVEN'T SEEN DR. 'Call me Gary' Markham since he took my stories away to read. No one has told me why he hasn't come back, but a nurse returned my notebooks to me. They were left in my room while I was at breakfast one day. No comment was ever made; they just appeared there in a Tesco carrier bag on my bed. I sometimes wonder what he thought, but then my head becomes too full of ideas and I forget he ever existed.

> *There is a man who wears a raincoat made of newspapers, but the papers are tomorrow's papers and he could tell the future by reading his coat, but he has never been able to read*

Other doctors have been to see me. There was one male doctor who was so tall that when he tried to sit, it was like watching a penknife being folded. Another was a woman who looked like an owl in a trouser suit and kept forgetting my name. And I thought owls were supposed to be wise. There hasn't been one of them who has come back twice; once seems to be their limit. There is obviously something about me that they don't want to see again, and I'm not sure if I am too mad for them or not mad enough. None of them seemed as keen as Markham to read my stories, though, which is a pity because I have so many stories to tell.

There is a house in which all the corridors and staircases lead only to the kitchen, and the table in the kitchen is always laden with wonderful food so that you have to eat every time you go in there until you are found one day blocking a corridor bloated and dead

I get by on less than two hours of sleep these days. Some nights, I don't sleep at all, but I never feel tired. My brain is so full of stories I don't think I could sleep any longer even if I wanted to. One day I'll be dead, and then I might stop, but in the meantime, there is so much to do and so little time.

Cats don't like to look into your eyes because they don't want you to know what they are thinking, that they are remembering the days when they were revered as gods and are plotting and waiting for the day when they will make us worship them again

They tried to take away my writing materials. I fought them, but I have always abhorred physical violence, and my lack of experience in such matters made it too easy for them to subdue me. They injected me with something, and I could only lie on my bed, battling sleep and watching as they took away my notebooks and pens. They soon returned them, however, when I bit open my fingertip and started to write on the walls in my blood. Now they leave me alone most of the time, except to deliver fresh notebooks and pens when I demand them, and meals that I sometimes consume while I work. I don't stop to eat or rest. I write

and write
and write
and write
and write
and write
and write

ABOUT THE AUTHOR

Liverpool born Bob Stone is an author and bookshop owner. He has been writing for as long as he could hold a pen and some would say his handwriting has never improved. He is the author of two self-published children's books, *A Bushy Tale* and *A Bushy Tale: The Brush Off*. *Missing Beat*, the first in a trilogy for Young Adults, was his first full-length novel and was followed by *Beat Surrender* and *Perfect Beat*, completing the trilogy. A complementary novella *Out of Season* was first published in the Beaten Track anthology *Seasons of Love* and then as a paperback in its own right. Since then he has had a children's picture book, *Faith's Fairy House*, published by Beaten Track and self-published his first adult novel *Letting the Stars Go*.

Bob still lives in Liverpool with his wife and cat and sees no reason to change any of that.

BY THE AUTHOR

Children's Fiction

A Bushy Tale

A Bushy Tale: The Brush Off

Faith's Fairy House

Young Adult Fiction

Missing Beat

Beat Surrender

Perfect Beat

Adult Fiction

Out of Season

The Custodian of Stories

Letting the Stars Go

BEATEN TRACK PUBLISHING

For more titles from Beaten Track Publishing,
please visit our website:

https://www.beatentrackpublishing.com

Thanks for reading!